My Starry Valentine

My Starry Valentine

A SWEET EX-MILITARY MOUNTAIN MAN ROMANCE

VALENTINE'S SWEETHEARTS

E.B. SILVA

The Valentine's Sweethearts Series

Check Out the Remaining Books in
the Valentine's Sweethearts Series

The "Valentine's Sweethearts" series is a collection of 18
heartwarming clean romance stories as sweet as a box of
chocolates. Featuring popular tropes such as fake dating,
friends to lovers, grumpy sunshine, accidental marriages,
opposites attract, love at first sight, and so much more!
Fate brings together couples who discover that true
connection goes beyond sweet nothings printed on candy. As
they navigate the season of love and their own hesitations, they
learn that sometimes, all it takes is one heartfelt message to
change everything.

"Valentine's Sweethearts" - Where love is in the air, and
romance blooms sweeter than candy hearts!

CHECK OUT THE REST OF THE SERIES HERE

Contents

Chapter 1   1
Ledger

Chapter 2   8
Luna

Chapter 3   15
Ledger

Chapter 4   20
Ledger

Chapter 5   25
Luna

Chapter 6   29
Luna

Chapter 7   35
Ledger

Chapter 8   43
Luna

Chapter 9   50
Luna

Chapter 10   58
Ledger

Chapter 11   66
Luna

Chapter 12   74
Ledger

Chapter 13   83
Luna

Also by E.B. Silva   93
About the Author   95

Chapter One
LEDGER

My Jeep dashboard flashes eight in the morning and a blustery twenty-three degrees. I take another swig of coffee with cream, staring up at the towering white frozen waterfalls of the Ouray Ice Park and the familiar green "Climber Only Area" and white and red "Crampons and a Helmet Required Beyond This Point" signs. Savoring the heat blasting from my vehicle's air vents, I only remove the key from the ignition when Chuck pulls up next to me in his red Toyota 4Runner.

The tall, lanky, gray-haired local nods as he glances through the passenger window of his car. His stoic face betrays no hint of disgust as he takes in my scarred left side, oblivious to what most people either can't take their eyes off or avert them from.

Sometimes, being around him, I almost forget about what happened. Chuck has ice-climbed this park since it opened in the nineties, and over the past three years since my relocation, he's taught me everything I know about the sport. Without his friendship and kindness, I wouldn't be alive. A former Navy hospital corpsman, he understands my military past, injuries, and current situation better than anyone.

Nodding at him through the driver's side window, I put my coffee thermos back in the cupholder, stepping out into the frigid air. I exhale sharply as the chill slams into me despite wearing a toasty base and mid-layer. The icy wind slices into my face and neck, a wolf's bare teeth biting into my scarred, sensitive flesh. Opening the trunk of my Jeep, I hustle into my alpine jacket, beanie, and an extra layer of pants before losing any more heat from my core.

I bluster in his direction, "Move to Colorado for its sky-kissing elevations and pristine star viewing, they said... I dunno. La Jolla sounds mighty welcoming right about now."

"Good old San Diego!" he exclaims, rounding the back of his vehicle to wrap me in a bear hug. "All beachy and inviting until you set foot in the freezing Pacific!"

"There's a reason they train the Seals at Coronado." I laugh, patting his back heartily.

"Brings back memories of the Silver Strand. Did you ever run that race?"

I nod, feeling the pull from the tight, puckered skin on the left side of my body. "More times than I can count."

"You gonna do anything about those dreads, dude?" Chuck asks, pointing at my overgrown hair. "You've got to be the scruffiest Marine in Colorado."

I shrug, frowning. My hair may be shoulder-length and unkempt, but it's not dreadlocked. Tangled is a distinct possibility, though. I bite my tongue instead of mentioning the last hairdresser I went to. The poor woman nearly had a heart attack at the sight of my face. Chuck's already heard the story... And dwelling on the same thing makes me sound pathetic. The only one who hates pathetic more than Chuck is me.

"The weather forecast looks great for today. The temperature should rise in the early afternoon enough to soften up the ice. I figure the climbing conditions will be perfect. It's a good thing you're wearing hard-shell pants because it's going to get wet and drippy later."

"I figured."

"Glad we could fit this in today. It's all downhill after this afternoon, with an aggressive storm front predicted to blow in overnight. Just in time to ruin locals' weekend plans."

"Yep, I had to get this in even though—"

"Let me guess. You pulled another all-nighter?"

I frown. "Nah, I went to bed around three, three-thirty. So, I should be in fair form."

He laughs, moving to the back of the 4Runner to finish gearing up and grab his pack. I follow suit. "Enjoy those short sleeps while you can. Once you hit your sixties, you won't be able to breathe without a full six hours of shut-eye."

"I haven't slept that much since before the Marines."

His face tightens with concern, and a prick of guilt stings me, followed by anger. *Can't a guy joke around here?* The answer comes swiftly. *After what you've put Chuck through? No.*

My friend asks, "You having trouble with sleep again?"

I can't lie to the man, even though I know it would go a long way toward assuaging his worry. "PTSD's been kicking in again. Some pretty rough dreams about...you know...the accident and after..."

"You been keeping up with therapy and meds?"

"Kind of."

Chuck shakes his head disapprovingly.

"I hate how fuzzy they make me feel. Besides, this here's the best therapy."

"Agreed," he says with a half-hearted smile. "But promise you'll get back with your therapist. You don't want things to go south again..."

I nod, feeling like a wimp. By *south*, he means a couple of low points I've had over the years. Times when I questioned everything too much...even the utility of my existence.

"I know you think I'm silly, but I find that prayer goes a long way, too." He gives me a knowing nod.

I bite my tongue because I'm here for fun and camaraderie. But my soul screams. *If prayer works so well, how the heck did I end up like this? Why did my comrades die?* Lord knows my sweet, long-suffering mama raised enough prayers on my behalf. But it's a moot point with Chuck, so I let it go.

Slipping on my helmet and crampons, I grab my backpack filled with extra clothing, rope, a first-aid kit, food, and water. Attachment points lining the outside of the backpack house my ice axes, harness gear loops, extra crampons, and everything else I need should things get gnarly. Ice screws and draws, belays and carabiners, anchor material, and my bail kit round out the necessities.

Compared to my one hundred-pound combat rucksack in the Corps, the climbing pack weighs roughly twenty pounds less, a pleasant relief. Although I've stayed in shape over the years, I'm no twenty-one-year-old.

In the distance, the squeal of small children makes me grateful I already have my helmet on. Still, I keep my head angled so the kids won't get a visual of the bad side.

Chuck notices, drawing his lips into a thin line. "You know, they'll have to learn sooner or later that life's not all bubblegum and cotton candy. And real heroes don't always look like Superman."

"Maybe," I grumble. "But I get tired of being everybody's learning moment, day in and day out."

He nods grimly.

Even though I fight it, a memory sears my mind from four years ago on my way home to my mother's house in SoCal. I remember with perfect clarity the toe-headed girl in the

Houston airport. She couldn't have been more than five or six. But her large baby blues flashed panic at the sight of me. With a shaking finger, she pointed, asking loudly, "Mommy, who's that monster?"

Perhaps even worse than the girl's reaction proved her mother's response. Without explanation, she frantically scolded the kid, more conscious of me in earshot than helping her daughter process the gruesome visual. I don't blame her. In the same situation, who knows what I might have done *before*...

But her immoderate response inadvertently confirmed the child's worst fears. That I'm a monster so terrifying I shouldn't be discussed or acknowledged. Most people take a similar tack. After all, it's the polite thing to do—looking through me or past me, ignoring me, and making me feel non-existent.

"You given any thought to the route we're taking today?"

His question isn't an easy one. The ice park has something like two hundred different ice climbs and mixed-use trails. We've ticked them off one by one, ramping up the difficulty with each visit. "I say Tiddlywinks or Prof. Chaos. Thoughts?"

"You're looking for steep today, huh?"

"I'm up for it if you're up for it. Besides, I'd like to spend the afternoon doing something physical and mindless."

Chuck warns, "Those steep bits won't let you check out."

"Yep, all good. By mindless, I don't mean check out. In fact, checking out is exactly what I don't want to do right now."

He looks confused but doesn't ask. "Well, you're the one running on a few hours of sleep, so it's your choice."

We continue grunting and talking as we make our way to the massive frozen white falls, what locals refer to fondly as the "Mecca of Ice." The largest ice park in the world, it has a primordial, frozen-in-time quality to it. Something about it comforts me, reminds me that no matter what, nature's ultimately in control, and all of us pea-brained pipsqueaks are merely along for the ride...and to learn something, I guess? I haven't figured that part out yet.

A group of climbers already dangle halfway up Tiddlywinks, so Chuck nods towards Prof. Chaos. "You had any luck in the female department lately?" The gray-haired climber always asks me this, despite my answer having remained the same since meeting him.

"I know you're a perpetual romantic, Chuck. But some of us have to be realists here. As much as I'd like some human companionship, I gave up that notion the first time I did a VA mirror test. Seriously, who'd settle for an ugly mug like this?"

Chuck's face remains deadpan. "God makes somebody for everyone."

The hardest part of hanging out with my good friend is always hearing about God. Again, if some bearded dad in the sky cared so much about me and my future, why'd he scramble my face into unlovable chaos? Even the most understanding woman has her limits. Heck, I wouldn't hang out with myself if I could escape the reflection in the mirror.

Even worse, the bend of Chuck's head tells me it's time to pray. I begrudgingly echo his pose as he says, "Heavenly Father, protect us on our climb today, and keep all the stupid tourists in mind who will likely be caught off guard by the impending storm. Oh, and maybe consider sending a helpmate for my pain-in-the-butt climbing buddy here. Amen."

I shake my head, frowning. "Thanks for the prayer, I guess. But there'll be no romance for me. I'm happy with my single, no-holds-barred life." My words couldn't be further from the truth. Fortunately, my friend ignores them.

I add, "Besides, all I ever do is hang out at the ice park or my cabin watching the stars. He'd have to drop her out of the sky for me to meet someone new." The last statement's slightly exaggerated as I get groceries and supplies in town and am friendly with the more understanding locals. But in a city of just over nine hundred people, romantic options are non-existent, especially for gals who like a freak show.

Standing at the bottom of the massive curling formation of icicles, Chuck and I crane our necks as we plan our best route up. He whistles long and low, shaking his head. "Don't let that smooth spot up top fool you. It's slippery as they come. You're going to level up technique on this one today."

"Having second thoughts, Squid? It's okay if you want to sit this one out," I tease.

"Heck, no, Devil Dog," he grumbles, patting me hard on the back. "You ready?"

"Let's do this," I reply, taking a deep breath and tamping down the knot rising in my stomach. Fear and foreboding are good signs. They'll keep my adrenaline high and my brain and muscles working fast and well. And when I glance back over the edge at the finish, reveling at the progress I've made as an ice climber, the tendrils of anxiety twisting and turning inside will transform into hot, searing waves of exhilaration.

I'll give God one thing... He knew what He was doing when he invented Colorado mountain highs.

"I'm going wherever you're going," I reply emphatically, looking at my best friend, Naomi. We've spent the last week in Ouray, cross-country skiing, snowshoeing, and exploring the quaint town, only to have everything fall apart in one fateful moment.

Three search and rescue workers with Ouray Mountain Rescue embroidered on their beanies and coats kneel over my bestie, stabilizing and wrapping her catastrophically injured ankle.

Everything happened in the blink of an eye. She went down wrong in a field of icy boulders, her ankle collapsing outward. Instead of the bindings on her skis or the blades giving way, her bones and joint did.

"No, actually, you're going to return to your vehicle and meet us at the ER at Montrose Regional Health," a salt-and-pepper bearded paramedic directs, narrowing his eyes at me. He introduced himself earlier as Peter...or was it Philip? Something with a "P." I can't think straight, thanks to the adrenaline coursing through my body.

"Montrose? But isn't that like an hour from here?" I pant.

"Forty-five minutes. That said, the weather's taking a turn for the worse, so we suggest driving slowly and carefully. We don't need you two bunking at the hospital."

I squeeze Naomi's fingers, looking at her drained face and blue-tinged lips. She fell two hours ago. Fortunately, it was sunny this afternoon, and far easier to stay warm than the last half hour or so. In that span, the wind picked up, and the sky darkened. In the distance, nature's fury sits poised, ready to unleash its mighty, icy fury.

The blonde, with a heart-shaped face and no-nonsense accent straight out of Oklahoma, urges, "He's right, Luna. It makes more sense for you to get the car and head back into town. That way, you can check out of the inn, grab our luggage, and handle everything we need to do because I messed up our trip."

I shake my head emphatically, shushing her. "You didn't mess up anything. It's my fault for talking you into skiing today."

The mountain rescue guy who piped in before clears his throat, grumbling, "It's nobody's fault. Engaging in winter recreation in Ouray comes with natural risks. Ankle breaks are a common injury this time of year."

Another fat, hot tear slides down my cheek, and my reaction embarrasses me. Naomi is holding up better than me, and she's the one with the horrible injury.

"I'm not in any pain at the moment," she reassures, worrying her thick bottom lip. "And I can't think of a better place to fracture some bones...enveloped in the equivalent of a giant ice pack."

My stomach tightens, remembering the sickening snap and her impossible attempts to stand up. She said, "There's no strength in the joint, as if putting pressure on it will blow it out." I'll never forget the moment she removed her boot, and I got my first real visual of the damage... The sight will haunt

9

me to my dying day, and that's when I called emergency services.

I sniffle, trying to laugh half-heartedly. "Yeah, I guess you have a point."

Peter or Philip clears his throat, ordering, "Alright, ladies, time to say your goodbyes. Ms. Solace, are you good to get back to your car? It's just a half mile in that direction." He points.

The search and rescue crew sped to us in a LiteTrax with high ground clearance that only fits four people. Besides, I'm nearly at the trailhead, and it's well-trafficked and clearly marked, so getting back to where we parked is a no-brainer.

"Can you take her skis, or should I try to manage them?"

The man smiles grimly. We've got her skis, backpack, and gear. You worry about getting yourself safely off this mountain."

I nod, feeling my heart pound against my ribs. "I can do that."

Naomi laughs weakly. "Are you sure, babe? Because, as I remember, you used to get lost in the middle school hallway, and there were only one hundred and fifty students in the whole place."

The corners of my mouth turn down. "I did a lot of daydreaming in middle school."

"True." She reaches for my hand, squeezing it again. "Alright then. I'll see you later at the hospital."

"You're the bravest person I know," I say as the men hoist her stretcher, beelining for the LiteTrax, where she carefully dismounts and takes a seat. "See you soon. Thank you, Mountain Rescue!"

The men nod, and I watch the vehicle speed away in a cloud of snow, brokenhearted. I wince, inwardly willing Naomi's journey to the hospital will go as smoothly as possible.

My eyes flutter to the angry clouds drawing closer by the minute. The air feels thick and ominous, and the wind's angry whistling has replaced the idyllic chirping of winter birds. If cold could be an odor, it pervades my senses, pure, sterile, and angry, riding the insistent wind that slaps my cheeks.

Thankfully, I don't have to ski into the wind. Instead, it pushes me from the back, helping me cover the frozen distance to my white 2014 Subaru Outback at record pace. My knees shake as the adrenaline from earlier bottoms out, coupled with low blood sugar. I feel dehydrated, but the chill in the air and the queasiness of my roiling stomach push me forward without stopping for water.

I scold myself mentally to take better care of myself as my SUV comes into view. All I can think about is Naomi and getting to the hospital in Montrose.

The last stretch proves demanding as the wind picks up, whipping around me like a mini frosted tornado. My long brown locks smack against my cheeks, and I paw back the tresses with my gloves to see my way to the finish line.

Shards of wind-borne ice blast my cheeks, the frantic gusts pushing me into the vehicle. I quickly remove my snow-encrusted gear and throw it in the back. Shivering and struggling with painfully numb fingers, I fasten my skis in place on the roof rack.

When I climb into my car and turn the key, massive tremors rock my core. I shiver in the driver's seat, frantically blowing warm air into my cupped hands as the car heater goes from cold to lukewarm and finally deliciously toasty.

The white accumulation on the window remains fresh and unpacked, so I don't have to scrape my windshield and windows. Instead, I turn on the wipers, letting the swish-swish restore my visibility. Rolling down the windows clears more of the white blur.

Putting the vehicle into four-wheel drive, I back up tentatively before inching forward and starting my descent along the forest service road toward the quaint alpine town of Ouray. Snowflakes swirl frantically around the car, smashing into my windshield and creating a strange gravity-less feeling. My eyes wander, following individual snowflake trails, and I squint hard, trying to make out road markers, signs, or other indicators I'm on the correct route.

The white whirlwind blinds me with its brightness still half-lit by brazen sunshine as shadows from the storm creep over my vehicle. My heart pounds in my chest, and I turn the radio down with shaking hands, uncertain where I'm at or where to go. My throat thickens as I ease my foot onto the brake pedal, and the tires slide and slip, struggling for purchase. The brakes automatically pump under my foot, announcing the treacherous slipperiness of the driving conditions.

Fortunately, I've driven on enough ski and snowshoeing trips to understand the basics of safe winter driving. It's certainly not something I learned growing up in the California Bay Area. But despite experience, the current conditions are what I'd term undrivable. According to the last forecast I saw, these driving conditions will only get worse. So time is of the essence for getting to Montrose.

Pumping my brakes to come to a gentle stop, I program my navigation system for the fastest route into town, feeling a little stupid about the whole thing. After all, Ouray boasts less than one thousand residents. It shouldn't be difficult to navigate its tiny network of roads. But visibility's approaching zero as the angry wind howls around my vehicle.

I pray under my breath as I watch the massive snowflakes pelt the car and pile up on the hood. I wonder how Naomi and her rescuers are faring.

Taking a deep breath, I put my car into drive again and move forward slowly, reminding myself that any progress is better than no progress. "You've got this, Luna." I remember the insane driving conditions I experienced while living and working in Baker, Nevada, outside my favorite national park, Great Basin, last spring. Still, nothing tops this ivory nightmare.

Suddenly, the pale, twisting flakes give way to a large, dark object, and I hit the brakes reflexively despite knowing better. Everything happens too fast. The wheels lock up despite four-wheel drive, and the vehicle spins around backward. I slide slowly but sickeningly, dropping down with a nauseating thud over the embankment, facing the wrong direction. The windshield wipers swish-swish as I clutch my chest, trying to catch my breath and slow my pounding pulse.

At first, my mind refuses to register the situation. Instead, I shift into drive, trying to climb out of the ditch. The disheartening sound of rubber on slick ice greets me as my wheels polish the surface below them smooth, unable to achieve friction. I press my foot to the metal again and again, countless times, driven by panic...until logic sinks in. "You're stuck, Luna. Like stuck stuck."

Sitting there shaking, I grab my purse on the passenger seat next to me, my hands and arms still trembling with adrenaline. Locating my cell phone, I pull it out to a screen with no bars. Fear transforms into anger as I pound the steering wheel and dash, screaming in frustration. Because of the events earlier with Naomi, I have less than no energy left, finally laying my head on the steering wheel and sobbing quietly.

I have no idea how long I do this. But snow buries my car, and my windows fog over from my breathing. Suddenly, a little voice inside my head commands, "Go up top for a signal. Get help."

Usually, I'm not one to listen to disembodied commands. But looking around, I admit I can't stay here any longer. If I do, I'm going to freeze to death. So, I jump out of my vehicle, slamming the door behind me. Wading through snow above my knees, I scramble up the embankment my car toppled down like an earthworm crawling on a wet sidewalk. It's not a pretty sight, but the exertion warms me quickly. Cresting the top of the trench, I let out a desperate cry as a silent world of infinite white greets me.

Snowflakes pile on my head, and my tears freeze on my cheeks as I search for landmarks or indicators of where I am. Looking abjectly at my phone, I still see no signal. The tiny, stupid voice was wrong. I let out another scream soaked in frustration. If I live a hundred years, I never want to see Ouray again.

Suddenly, in the distance, I hear engine noises and snow crunching beneath tires. It's faint but consistent. Holding my breath to stop my noisy panting, I strain my ears, listening again. It's still there. Only a little louder now.

My breath rattles in my throat. "Oh, please. Oh, please." I don't even know what I'm begging for because I'm unsure what I hear. All I know is any noise is better than the raging swirl of this blizzard. And then, I see it—a snow-crusted, dark gray, lifted, Jeep Wrangler inching its way in my direction.

Letting out a cry of joy, I wave my hands frantically in the air, desperate to get the driver's attention.

Chapter Three

LEDGER

The petite feminine form in the road draws the breath from my chest and makes my throat thick and tight. Scanning the area around her, I don't see any cars. *Where did she come from?* My brain taunts me, revisiting the earlier conversation with Chuck. *She dropped from the sky...* I frown. *Whatever.*

The woman wears an olive drab and rose pink-lined Columbia jacket with brown and gray fur trimming the hood, a pair of black ski pants, and a pair of gray, fur-trimmed Sorel snow boots that stop two inches below her knees.

Her silky, curly brown locks reach to her middle back, whipping around thanks to her frantic movements and the wild gusts from the blizzard. Once I reach her, stopping carefully and rolling down my window, the sight of her face socks me hard in the chest and the gut.

My eyes meet hers like a physical collision, a sharp exhale escaping my lips. I notice with unexpected satisfaction the puff of air that leaves her mouth, too. The feeling is akin to static electricity, shocking my hand as I touch a doorknob after walking over thick carpet. Only soul-shaking and visceral.

Her brows jump in her forehead, and her eyes round. She feels it, too. And it isn't just her getting a load of my bad side. Habit has made me scrupulous about how to hold my head to spare people that visual. But I can't hide in plain sight like this forever, which makes whatever alchemical reaction going on between us a problem. A big, big problem.

Nevertheless, I absorb her impossible beauty, instantly breathless and stunned that someone like her exists. Suddenly, my experience on this planet feels worthwhile, though I know she can never be mine. Still, sharing the same air space is something—a pretty impressive something that will stick with me for a long time.

I can't help myself, smiling like an idiot as my eyes glide down her oval, symmetrical face. They dance over her sassy, slightly upturned nose and settle on her full, rich, rose-colored lips.

Did I say static electricity before? No, this is lightning, and I'll never be the same.

"Thank God!" she exclaims, her face beaming, and I'm about to be a believer if things keep up this way. At a bare minimum, I'm staring at an angel...a glowing one with an ear-to-ear grin and a full set of pearl-white teeth. "You are the most beautiful sight I've seen all day!" She exclaims enthusiastically.

And it's confirmed... I'm having a heart attack...and a near-death experience all rolled into one because those words from those lips in that silky voice. It's too much... Clouds could part and trumpets sound, and it wouldn't impress me as much as devouring this woman's face with my eyes. Before I can get a hold of myself, I reply breathlessly, "And you're the most beautiful sight I've seen...maybe ever."

Her grin widens, if that's possible, and I feel like time is frozen. But it can't be because a storm pounds around us, and the wind howls. The cab of my vehicle shakes, and I rudely awaken to the present reality. Only the stunning angel remains...

Which leads to immediate, intense self-consciousness and loathing. I push my hair over my bad side more thoroughly. "Why are you here?"

Her lips part, and she stares at me long and hard. I know my rugged appearance is off-putting, but she's out of options for assistance. Ouray's local monster, it is. "M-m-my car...I drove into a tree or a ditch or something, and now I'm stuck and can't get out."

I eye her carefully, trying to keep the scarred part of me out of her line of sight. But nothing has changed. She still steals my breath and makes my heart clobber illogically against the interior wall of my ribcage. She's the kind of girl I would have enthusiastically flirted with in my former life. I can tell by the flush of her cheeks and the way her eyes rove over the good parts of me, she would have flirted back. I remind myself that one sharp turn, one sweep of my long hair away from my face will transform the angel's ambivalent expression into one of horror.

Clearing my throat, I growl, "Have you called emergency services yet?"

She shakes her head emphatically, cocking her head to the side and eyeing me suspiciously. It must be starting to sink in that I don't look at her head-on. "No, I was just about to when I heard your Jeep. I figured live help is worth more than a voice over the phone...if I can get a voice over the phone. I don't have a cell phone signal here."

"It could be tricky with this storm. But you should always be able to call 911 because emergency service calls go to the first available cell phone tower, no matter your service provider. However, your emergency isn't necessarily 911 level now that I've found you."

"Y-y-yes," she stammers breathlessly. I sense a new hesitant

17

energy as she weighs the dangers of staying versus the risks of me."That's why hearing the engine of your vehicle was a miracle."

"I'm no miracle, ma'am. But I do know one thing. Emergency services will be taxed thanks to this storm, blowing in fast and hard. Heck, I'll be lucky if I make it back to my cabin. I could give you a lift in that direction, though, until the storm blows over. I've got food, heat, and a satellite phone you're welcome to use. And I'm not a creep, serial killer, or anything like that, although..." I pause for a long moment, trying to figure out how to say this. "I'm hard on the eyes."

Her brows furrow, and confusion floods her face.

I grimace, imagining how her countenance will tighten when she gets a good view of my face. I can already hear the hiss of air from her lungs as she tries to act like nothing's wrong.

The lovely woman cranes her neck some more. Wagging her head back and forth between her car crashed in the ditch next to us and my vehicle, she observes, "I see you're a Marine?" She points towards the sticker in the Jeep's back window.

"Yes, ma'am."

She presses her lovely pink lips firmly together. "My grandpa was a Marine. A Vietnam veteran... Well, seeing as I'm kind of out of options, I would appreciate a lift..."

"Normally, I'd offer to drive you into town. But this storm looks bad. A few more minutes talking, and we both might end up stuck along this road."

"Okay," she says, breathlessly.

I nod, frowning deeply. "In that case, let's get this over with."

She raises her eyebrows quizzically as I pull the e-brake and hop out, rounding the front of the Jeep. I don't know any other way to do this than quickly and decisively like pulling off a bandage. As soon as I reach where she stands, her big brown eyes tick to my scars, only semi-hidden by my hair blowing in the wind.

Her expression goes instant deer-in-headlights, although she has far more self-control than most people the first time they see me. Her calm, clinical examination reminds me a little of how Chuck regards me. I fight the urge to apologize for my looks. Chuck pointed out a long time ago how weird and awkward that is. Besides, I have no words, my heart aching acutely in my chest, as her face strains, trying not to register the shock and horror her vision bestows.

C learing my throat, I inquire gruffly, "What do you need to get out of your car?"

"Oh, yes..." she says, turning back towards the embankment where I see faint glimmers of earlier tire treads. She definitely went a way cars are not supposed to go. "I guess just my purse, phone, and backpack. I also have extra food and water in the car, if you think we could use it?"

"We'll bring it all. Better to hope for the best and prepare for the worst."

She smiles, nodding. "My grandpa always says that." As we work to remove items from her snow-covered car, hopelessly sunk in the ditch, I appreciate her lithe, athletic movements. Clearly, she feels comfortable in snowy surroundings. Retrieving her purse, extra jacket, backpack, and food and water, I hear the click of her locking car door.

"I doubt you'll have too many people around here trying to steal your car in the middle of a blizzard," I grumble. I don't need to point this out, and I'm not sure why I do. But it does darken her cheeks, which does more crazy stuff to my heart. I wasn't lying when I told her she's the most beautiful creature I've seen in a long time. Maybe ever.

Shrugging, she says, "Force of habit. I'm from the Bay Area."

I nod. "I get it. I'm from San Diego."

"Of course you are," she replies, chuckling softly.

"Why do you say that?"

"A Marine with long hair? Where else would you find that but San Diego?"

I chuckle at the preposterousness of her statement. "Nowhere if you're active duty... I guess unless you're a spook or something." I scream over the raging wind, opening the Jeep door for her. She piles inside, and I fight the urge to lean forward and buckle her in. *You're not on a date, dummy.*

Shutting the door behind her, I round the Jeep carefully to avoid slipping in the snow. Jumping back in, I shift into gear, removing the brake with a click. The wind whips so violently around us now that the vehicle shudders, and I take it slow, crunching along the white lane at a snail's pace to make out where we're headed.

"Can you see the road?" she asks in a croaking little voice, leaning forward and narrowing her eyes.

"I'm watching the trees, the boulders, the curves of the embankment that I can make out... Fortunately, I know Ouray like the back of my hand."

"How? I thought you said you were from San Diego," she challenges, putting a warmth in my chest I don't recognize. It's been a long time. I mean, a really long time since a beautiful woman wanted to know anything about me.

"My grandpa lived up here. I own his cabin now." The words come out slowly and grumpily as I concentrate on where to steer my tires.

"Unlike me, who drove into the first ditch I could find..."

"A lot of drivers have trouble with that bend," I grumble,

my hands squeezing the steering wheel so tightly my knuckles turn white. The conversation dies off after that as we both settle into the direness of our situation. I wasn't joking when I said we could end up stuck, too. Fortunately, we have her extra food and water with us. But escaping bigger concerns, like freezing to death, could be problematic.

The woman swallows loudly next to me. She smells of lavender and roses, and I marvel at the strange contrast of her springtime fragrance with the barren, bleakness of this wintry landscape.

She clears her throat, saying in a smooth voice, "You're doing good."

The words may be few and simple. But they make my chest swell with pride. A visceral part of me, deep down in the core of my being, longs to protect and care for her. To keep her safe at all costs. The feeling both scares and thrills me.

She asks, "What's your name?"

"Ledger Brooks."

"I'm Luna Solace," she replies.

I nod, biting my tongue hard. Strange thoughts swirl in my head. *That's a beautiful name, Luna. But not as beautiful as you. Luna and Ledger. They sound good together.* I don't know what it is about the angel seated beside me that turns me into a lovestruck teen.

Concentrate on getting her safely to your cabin, Ledger. Don't mess this up. Or two people could end up trapped in a blizzard tonight.

"And what were you doing today, Ledger, before you stumbled across me?"

"Ice climbing at the park."

"Ice climbing? You're one of those guys?" She pronounces the words with awe, making me feel like an instant celebrity.

I nod. "Does that surprise you?"

She looks at me long and hard, focusing on my right bicep,

squeezed into my tight-fitting mid-layer. "Not at all. Ice climbing is really impressive. I could never do it."

I shake my head, entirely unconvinced by her proclamation. "You could. I've seen plenty of women out there."

She shivers next to me. "Yeah, but I'm not a fan of heights."

"Some of the best climbers in the world—whether ice or rocks—are afraid of heights."

"There's no way," she counters, shaking her head.

"Yes, way. I can show you a couple of climbers like that if we have internet at the cabin. Satellite can be spotty up here, even in decent weather."

She nods skeptically, eyeing me with an expression that feels an awful lot like admiration. If I'm not careful, I could get used to the glow it inspires in me from the inside out.

At the top of my mountain, I breathe a sigh of relief. Snowflakes dance frenetically, closing us in and inspiring a claustrophobic disorientation. My nine thousand-foot views are non-existent in this thick, wintry weather—the visual consistency of potato soup. "My cabin's a couple hundred feet that way, although you'd never believe it in this weather."

A sharp sigh graces her lips. "Finally, something going right today," she whispers. I can tell by the tired tone of her voice that she has a lot more to say, and I celebrate being counted among the "something going right" parts of her life.

I want to sit her down, hold her hands, and stare lovingly into her face while asking about her day. I'll never do this in real life, of course. I can't begin to count the endless ways my appearance has stilted my responses to other people, rendering me a heartless-seeming bystander.

"Watch your step," I caution as I wade around the Jeep to help her down. She grabs my arm for support, and the skin sizzles on the back of my hand where her petal-soft fingertips inadvertently brush my flesh. *Lightning. Again.*

After more than five years without female companionship, the gesture feels akin to nirvana. Delicious sparks feather across the flesh of my arm, shooting up its length to my heart. The breath rattles in my throat despite my best efforts to play it cool, and my cheeks heat.

Get control of yourself, man. You're a thirty-nine-year-old Marine, not a kid with a schoolboy crush. I securely place my other hand atop hers, and she smiles warmly, melting my heart. I walk her toward my front porch, shrouded in the fluffy white veil of the storm, working hard not to hyperventilate.

"Let's get you safely inside, and then I'll grab the rest of your stuff."

"Thank you," she says softly, and I'm aware of her eyes roving over my profile. I bring my head forward, shaking it slightly to ensure my hair fully shrouds my bad side.

Luna lets out a tiny puff of air as her boots slip out from under her, and she nearly takes a tumble. But I hold onto her securely, steadying her.

"It's more slippery than it looks," she observes, leaning in to wrap her left arm tightly around my waist. The move sends electric shocks straight to my core, and I breathe hard despite being well-acclimated to the elevation.

As soon as we stand inside the entryway, her arm falls away. I feel instantly and entirely alone again. More lonely than before ever meeting her. *What has she done to me in the short time since I found her standing in the road?* Not ready to think this through any further, I excuse myself back outside to grab the rest of her belongings, ducking my head away from her inquisitive gaze.

Chapter Five

LUNA

I can still feel the warmth of Ledger's muscular body on my arm and side as he turns on his heels, heading back toward the front door with a grumble. "Make yourself at home. I'll get the rest of your stuff."

I admire him from behind, his physique large and muscular, at well over six feet tall. He's got the build and perfect posture of a Marine. The angry red scars on the left side of his face, which he tries to conceal with his long hair, make me think he's a wounded warrior.

Of course, I shouldn't jump to any conclusions, but it's clear he's been burned. By his mannerisms, it's also obvious he's attracted to me and feels uncomfortable with me in his space. I wonder if this has to do with his appearance or something else.

There's no telltale wedding band on his left hand, but after taking off my snow boots and setting them on the mat near the front door, lined with man-sized snow and work boots, I walk around his cabin slowly, looking for signs of a wife or children. Instead, I find the accouterments of a cowboy. A rack lined with Stetsons in various shades and

25

hand-tooled, well-worn leather boots in the line by the front door.

The living room includes an impressive hearth constructed from local granite, which complements the rich, dark tones of the expertly finished wood lining the walls and floors. Ledger meant it when he said cabin, and I admire the beautiful Persian rugs covering the floor and imbuing the chilly air with a sense of warmth. I can only imagine how cozy this place will feel with a roaring fire.

Rustic, rough-hewn, wood-framed couches invite visitors to sit on overstuffed leather cushions lined with tribal-patterned accent pillows. I don't know if the designs are Native American or from farther afield, like the rich rugs.

The back corner of the room draws my eyes to a modest memory box containing a photograph of a breathtakingly handsome, clean-cut Marine. The youth and lack of scars, long hair, and beard veil his identity, making me scrutinize the image closely. But I recognize Ledger in the kind, sky-blue eyes and rugged square-cut jawline.

The box also contains a smaller candid photo of him in full camo and gear overseas with his firearm. The background is orange and sandy. I can't tell if it's Iraq, Afghanistan, or elsewhere. Besides photos, there are a handful of medals, including a purple heart. The last time I saw the glittery memento with George Washington's profile in relief was as a little girl, stealing a forbidden glance into my grandpa's top bedroom drawer where he keeps his most sacred possessions.

The front door flies open, and the whistle of the blizzard fills the room with a burst of cold air. I turn around, my face heated with guilt, feeling like a voyeur caught mid-gaze. My eyes lock with Ledger's intensely blue ones for the briefest of moments, and it hits me again. The inexplicable zing of electricity crackling in the air between us.

But then, he turns again, shrouding his left side in hair and shadows and breaking the moment. It's awkward how he tries to veil the painfully obvious, though I saw his scars as we unloaded my car.

His refusal to make full eye contact feels oddly dismissive, though unintended. I can't shake the inexplicable sense of familiarity between us. Like I know him from somehow or, at a bare minimum, *should* know him. The strangeness of this sentiment sparks irrational frustration as he continues to hide from me, physically and emotionally.

"There's a guest bedroom in the back, where I'll put your stuff. I'm sure you don't want to hear this, but I think you're more or less stuck here. At least for the night. The weather's pretty crazy outside."

His words don't surprise me, but I still let out a tired little sigh, struggling to grasp the craziness of the day. His shoulders hunch as he walks past, and he says under his breath, "I'm sorry to relay the bad news to you. I'm sure you have other places you need to be. But in Ouray, nature always gets the first say."

"It's not that," I call after him, kicking myself for seeming ungrateful. "I've just had the most insane day ever. And yes, there is somewhere I really need to be."

He pauses at the sound of my voice, listening attentively without turning. "I'm sorry," he says before disappearing down the hallway.

In his absence, I go back to surveying the room. Black and white Ansel Adams photographs line the walls, and the cabin has a large open-air plan with a skylight punctuating vaulted ceilings. It must be glorious on summer days, but now it amplifies the wildness of the storm outside. The sky looks angry and dark overhead, and I imagine my host is optimistic in his forecast that I might have to spend one night here. It doesn't look like this blizzard will let up any time soon.

The Marine strides back into the room, his perfect posture

restored and that contagious energy rolling off him that drew me to him during the Jeep ride. I can tell he's a man who enjoys life, savors it to the best of his ability despite the cards dealt him. It's an odd and alluring juxtaposition against the severe nature of his disfigurement.

He turns to the side again, not making eye contact with me, and I hate it. I hate the fact I make him uncomfortable in his own home, and I hate that he feels the need to conceal his scars from me.

But I don't know him well enough to know how to proceed. My gut tells me to be forthright and state the obvious. But for some wounded warriors, this may be an unforgivable sin. I know this because my grandfather was a double amputee, and many veterans injured in combat visited our house.

Grandpa lost both legs to a landmine and spent most of his life working from a wheelchair because he found prosthetics uncomfortable. As much as he never let his injuries keep him down, he also despised people talking about them. I wouldn't call him a proud man, but he told me once that he was tired of his missing legs being the icebreaker for every conversation with every person on the planet. I wonder if Ledger feels the same way.

Chapter Six

LUNA

Ledger's rich, masculine voice draws me back from my thoughts. "Excuse my poor manners. I don't get a lot of guests up this way. May I offer you something to drink or eat? Beer and pizza, maybe?"

"What kind of beer?"

"A variety of local brews," he says. "You'll have to check out the fridge if you're picky."

"I'm not picky as long as they're not too hopsy."

"So, no IPAs. I think I can swing that."

"Thank you."

The corners of his mouth turn up almost imperceptibly, although his gaze remains trained ahead as he strides past me into the kitchen. "There's a bathroom down the hallway with towels and everything you need for a shower. Please make yourself at home."

My heart pounds against my ribs as I take in his handsome, rugged profile. Squeezing my hands tightly together, I say, "You mentioned something about a satellite phone. Is that something I could use before I take a shower? Because I'm supposed to be at the hospital right now, and the last thing I want is everyone worrying about me when I don't show up."

"The hospital?" he asks, his brows knitting together.

"Yes, my best friend Naomi and I were out cross-country skiing today when there was a terrible accident..." The tremble in my voice stops me.

He moves a step closer to me, turning ever so slightly to make eye contact with me and giving me the slimmest glimpse of his injured side.

"Yes, she broke her ankle, and it took hours for search and rescue to get to us." I bite my lower lip, holding back a sob.

"How bad was the break?" he asks, frowning.

"It was a compound fracture."

He grimaces, moving closer until he stands in front of me. He hesitates before tentatively touching my upper arm and rubbing it reassuringly. My heart pounds wildly, my flesh igniting beneath his fingers despite the thin layer of sleeve between us.

"How did she get to the hospital?"

"The plan was Ouray Mountain Rescue would take her by LiteTrax down the mountain, and I'd meet her at the hospital in Montrose. So, if I could use your satellite phone, it would be appreciated."

"Of course," he says, letting his hand drop as he sweeps past me into the kitchen, grabbing a black device from the top of the fridge. As he hands the bulky phone to me, our fingers accidentally brush, making my cheeks burn and a muscle jump along his square-cut, bearded jawline.

Looking down at the screen and buttons, I freeze. "I've never used a satellite phone before. Can you help me?"

"Sure. We have to bundle back up and head outside, though."

After quietly putting our coats and boots on, Ledger offers his arm, leading me into the blizzard until we find a clear spot, or at least what he says would be a clear spot, if it wasn't storming. I'm skeptical the phone will work in this weather, but he reassures me it will.

He talks me through turning it on, extending the antenna, and waiting for a connection. I dial Naomi's cell phone number. Five call attempts later, she finally answers.

"Babe, what number are you calling me from? Where are you?" Her voice sounds surprised and relieved.

I plug my ear, yelling over the blizzard's gusts. "I got stuck in the blizzard driving back to Ouray. But this nice cowboy-mountain-man rescued me. I'm safe now, but this weather's awful. So, don't expect me to make it to Montrose anytime soon. What are they saying about your ankle?"

"Okay, wait a sec..." she says, clearing her throat. "What's a cowboy-mountain-man, and is he cute?"

Her question makes me painfully aware of the big Marine standing a little distance away but still within hearing range. "I'll explain later, and yes. Very much so."

"Oh my goodness!" she squeals into the phone far more enthusiastically than she should.

"What kinds of meds do they have you on, Nana?" Nana is one of many nicknames I have for my bestie.

"The good stuff. But enough about me. I want to hear more about this cowboy-mountain-man of yours."

"Not mine, and it's complicated. But no worries. I'll fill you in on the details later." I repeat the question she previously ignored. "What are they saying about your ankle?"

She sighs long and hard. "I need surgery. That's all I know for sure. Oh, and I'm in room two seventy-six."

"Surgery? Oh my gosh, Naomi, have you called your parents to let them know yet?"

"Yep, and they're freaking out. Trying to find the fastest tickets out of Oklahoma City to Colorado. They finally get to

31

have their Rocky Mountain adventure...only not under the best circumstances."

"I'm glad they're on their way, and I'll be there as soon as I can. But this weather needs to let up, and I need to figure out what's going on with my car and get our stuff out of the hotel room."

"Yep..."

A tinge of selfishness pricks me. Why am I telling her this on the eve of surgery? She has vastly more important things to focus on. "But don't you worry about any of that. Just focus on getting better. Promise?"

"Pinkie promise... This goes without saying, I hope. But focus on your cowboy-mountain-man."

I blush. "It's not what you think. I'll explain later."

"Can I call you back at this number?" she asks.

I look at Ledger, catching him staring at me. "Can Naomi call me back on this line if need be?"

"Yes, although we'll likely only see the call after the fact. She can text the number, too."

"Oh, he has a sexy voice," she croons.

I frown. "Maybe your doctor needs to tone down your meds."

"It's Valentine's Day, babe. At least one of us should enjoy a little romance..." Her voice cracks. Oh no. This is far worse than her teasing me about Ledger. The floodgates open, and I try to comfort her, shushing and whispering reassuring words. "A broken ankle on Valentine's Day? What's the universe trying to tell me?"

"Maybe to marry an orthopedic surgeon? Or a mountain rescue guy?"

She chuckles, and I sigh, relieved.

"You know, my surgeon is pretty cute, babe..."

"Talk about a dramatic way to meet someone..." The

Marine shoots me a dark glance, and I wonder what he's thinking based on the one-sided conversation.

"But enough silliness. Yes, you can call this number, but bear in mind a few things..." I quickly relay the information from Ledger to my bestie about the satellite phone, my teeth chattering as he patiently waits. I finish with a quick prayer at Naomi's request and end the call.

I hand the phone to Ledger, and he takes my arm, leading me towards his porch again. "A cowboy-mountain-man?" he grumbles with a frown. "Is that a good thing?"

I smile up at him, calling over the storm, "Between the boots, the hats, the cabin, and the elevation, it's accurate. But I apologize for making assumptions. What would you call yourself?"

He shrugs, looking the most relaxed I've seen since our meeting, despite the chilly breezes hammering us and intermittently uncovering the part of his face he works so hard to hide. "A hick astronomer."

"An astronomer?" I ask, my eyes rounding.

A surprisingly gorgeous laugh escapes his lips. "Why does that surprise you?"

"I've never met an astronomer before," I confess as he opens the front door for me.

"It's a geeky profession," he declares gruffly.

"I think geeks are hot," I flirt, side-eyeing him.

"Said nobody ever..." he adds with a frown.

"I'm not nobody, Starboy," I reply, raising my chin in challenge.

"That's for sure," he concedes, his voice dropping in timbre, appraising me more boldly as we stand by the welcome mat, removing our boots and coats. "Starboy? What's up with all the name-calling?"

I shrug. "You need a nickname or two."

"And you're the woman who's going to give them to me?"

I shrug again, pursing my lips. "Maybe." He smiles broadly, distracted enough to forget about hiding his scars from me momentarily.

This feels good, the chemistry zinging between us. I could get used to this heady feeling.

"It's a shame you showed up during a blizzard. Because on a clear night, I could give you the show of your life," he says, pointing skyward. "This part of Colorado boasts some of the most pristine night skies in the world."

"Really? I would love to see them."

"Maybe we'll get lucky, and the storm will break before you leave," he says with a nod. "Now, I've got a fire to get started and dinner to figure out while you relax and warm up."

Staring at this grumpy beast of a man with long, wild brown hair, a scruffy beard, piercing blue eyes, and a handsome, chiseled, frowning profile, he presents the ultimate mystery. Reclusive and smart, clearly self-conscious about his appearance, and attractive in a rugged, feral way that I have trouble defining or denying.

Chapter Seven

LEDGER

My angel excuses herself to the guest bedroom to freshen up, and I set up the bread machine to make pizza dough and start pre-warming the oven. Then, I head for my bedroom to get washed up. After a long day of ice climbing, I can only imagine how I smell and look.

I shower quickly, not allowing myself to stay long under the hot spray. But I find myself using the best shampoo and body wash combo I own. Something my mom bought me last Christmas. Something I was pretty sure was a total waste of her money.

Now, I thank the wise woman for her providential gift. Even when reality smacks me hard and ruthlessly upside the head. *Why would Luna care about how you smell? She's here against her will. And she'll leave as soon as the blizzard breaks.*

But the nasty inner critic can't drown out the pounding of my heart or how my mind flashes to all that's adorable about her—pretty much everything, as far as I can tell. The way she purses her full, kissable mouth while thinking deeply. How her eyes flutter up to the right as if searching the sky or ceiling for answers. The silkiness of her soft voice and how she squeezes her hands in front of her when she's nervous. The stunning arch of her eyebrows when she's curious. The pink flush of her cheeks when embarrassed...

I'm obsessed, and I've known her for less than one hour. Is this how moths feel pursuing the moon? If so, I'm ready to fly all night.

Maybe I indulge in these feelings and thoughts because it's been so long since I thought about loving or being loved. Maybe it's because I realize inherently the fleeting nature of this moment. After all, an insurmountable problem exists... one I can't ignore forever.

Time for a little mirror therapy. I start with the good side. The side that could almost convince me I'm worthy of love. It's not too shabby, even though wrinkles around my eyes and mouth attest to a life thoroughly lived. Then, with a grimace, I turn to the left. Flipping my hair back, I absorb the mass of red, shapeless scar tissue punctuated by my lashless blue eye.

I'm luckier than many burn victims. My nose and lips are intact. But my cheeks look angry and thick, and my left ear is little more than a melty lump. My beard doesn't grow on that side, except in weird little patches, and I have no eyebrow. I read somewhere that eyebrows are essential to facial recognition. Good luck with this hunk of flesh.

The scar tissue extends down one side of my neck, over my shoulder partway down my back and along an angry patch over my chest to where my abs start. It cuts more than one of my Marine tattoos in half, making my anchor, bulldog, and full-chest Sailor Jerry eagle ink look like fizzled-out kindergarten artwork. Some comrades in similar positions have suggested redoing the ink to fill in the missing areas and make my appearance more tolerable for others. But is "tolerable" a way to live a life?

The scar tissue and grafted skin feel tight, itchy, and hot to the touch in spots, and the colors vary from angry red to a pasty white, bumpy in some spots and pulled taut in others. Frigid temperatures slice through the damaged nerve endings like a butcher knife, and visions of me have made little kids and grown women cry.

How's that for a soulmate? I sigh long and hard, forcing myself to look and look and look...until I feel despondent.

The VA keeps trying to connect me with a facial reconstruction program out of UCLA that may be able to make me look more presentable, even create a prosthetic ear for me, and help me with eyebrow and beard implants. But I've already been through so many surgeries and endured so much pain. And in the name of what? To never recognize the patched-up person staring back at me.

Focusing on my lashless and eyebrowless left eye, I say out loud, "There's no way in hell Luna would ever be attracted to you. She's perfect. She deserves the best the world has to offer, not a burned-out shell of a man."

Never one to engage in self-pity for long, I keep the pathetic self-lecture brief. To my surprise, its after-effects are even shorter lived. Toweling off my hair, I dress quietly, my head buried in too many thoughts and feelings to sort out properly. Try as I might to convince my heart to take it down a notch, what I feel for this woman is undeniable.

What is harder to explain, though, are the looks she gives me in return. Breathless ones with a warmth simmering behind her eyes that I used to recognize but fear to acknowledge now.

Why me? Why a man disfigured past the point of recognition over one-third of his body?

But I've been down this road countless times, and I know hate-filled self-talk won't get me anywhere. Instead, I need to focus on action. In this case, whipping up the best pizza Luna's ever tasted. And finding a way to make my limited time with her unforgettable. If there's anything my thirty-nine years on this planet and near death have taught me, it's the precious and fleeting nature of life.

In the kitchen, I pull the raised pizza dough out of the bread machine, cut it in half, and place one round on a floured breadboard for kneading. Working the rubbery stuff to the perfect consistency, I spread it out on a large pizza pan before poking holes in the crust, sprinkling it with Italian seasoning, and popping it into the oven to bake.

"You are not!" I look up at the sound of Luna's silky voice, and a knot of desire lodges in my throat. I made an incalculably bad error by suggesting Luna borrow some of my clothes for after the shower. What else could I do, though?

The stunning brunette with snapping brown eyes swims in one of my olive-drab Marine sweatshirts that falls past her knees with sleeves hanging beyond her hands by several inches so she has to bunch up the ends. Coupled with gigantic, matching sweatpants rolled up a few times at the top and bottom, she swims in the layers. There's one massive problem with all of this: she looks like mine...

Mine, mine, mine.

And I like it way too much. Swallowing hard, I try not to devour her with my eyes, all the time feeling akin to the big, bad wolf.

"Hi," she says, blushing, and I realize how intently I'm staring.

Shaking my head and clearing my throat, I manage, "Am not what?"

"You are not making pizza from scratch."

I look down at my hands buried in another round of white dough and my apron covered in flour, scrunching my forehead. "Uhh...yeah, I am. Is that a problem?"

"Not at all. My grandparents—who I grew up with—

always had Saturday pizza night. And grandma insisted on making it from scratch, so this makes me feel right at home."

"Except it's Friday, not Saturday," I reply, shrugging and looking at my watch.

"You're right," she says. "And it's Valentine's Day, to boot."

A loud breath escapes my lungs, and I'm not entirely sure why. I guess because my body has decided to go all out and embarrass the heck out of me with my physical reactions around this woman. Fortunately, if she notices, she doesn't let on.

"I'm sorry I don't have flowers or chocolates for you," I growl. "But you kind of caught me off guard with your arrival. If I didn't know better, I'd swear you fell straight from the sky or something..." I bite my tongue before calling her *angel*. Thank goodness for one last modicum of self-control.

Luna's cheeks burn as she confesses, "I don't have anything for you either because you didn't even exist for me until an hour ago."

I shrug, feeling the heat of her gaze on my face. It occurs to me that I'm not really hiding my bad side from her anymore. Yet, no worry lines streak her face. No disgust tightens the muscles of her visage.

Honestly, she acts like speaking to me and looking at my half-melted face is the most natural thing in the world. She acts like she sees me for who I am without judgment, and it's dangerously addictive.

"If you're okay with local brews and homemade pizza, we've got the makings of a decent Valentine's Day. And we can stream movies, although by the looks of the weather, I may need to dust off the DVD player instead. But I've got enough old DVDs to get us by either way. You always have to be prepared for crazy weather up here. Maybe we can find something to watch that goes with the whole Valentine's Day theme. That is unless I'm making you uncomfortable with the holiday talk?"

"Do I look uncomfortable?"

I stop kneading the dough, shifting my weight and staring at her long and hard. "Not one bit," I whisper.

She doesn't even flinch as she returns my gaze.

The air feels sucked out of the room, and I fight hard to play it cool. "I guess what I mean to say is if you've got a boyfriend or fiancé, I should stop while I'm ahead. You know?"

"I don't have either," she says matter-of-factly.

Thank God.

"And why not?" The question escapes my lips before I can stop myself. But I can't help it. Luna not having a boyfriend is like the Earth having no gravitational pull.

She drops her head, her cheeks flushing. "Probably because most guys my age are pretty immature and unimpressive, especially compared to a guy like..." she stops abruptly, looking like the cat that swallowed the canary.

"Like?" I ask, wondering what she gets that I don't. I feel like I've been left out of an inside joke or something.

"Like you."

Is this woman trying to kill me? My heart performs a timpani solo that would make the Denver Symphony proud. I swallow hard, trying to give her a way out. "You're a bad liar, Luna."

"Liar?" Her voice cracks over the word, and I look up, shocked to see her face flushing. Maybe the misguided woman is sincere.

An acute ache pierces my chest, and deep discomfort grips me. "You need to get out more if you think I'm impressive," I grumble with a frown.

She presses her lips firmly together, staring at me long and hard. "What's there not to be impressed by? You're a Marine and an ice climber. You live in a cozy cabin on a Colorado peak, working as an astronomer. You wear cowboy hats and boots. You drive a massive Jeep that can basically power through any blizzard. You make pizza from scratch, and you appreciate local brews. Those are all impressive things, Ledger."

I shrug.

"You know, the ice climbing thing in particular is insane to me. I'm sure the fact I'm afraid of heights has something to do with it. But you guys are fearless. Since coming to Ouray, I've visited the park every chance I get, sitting there and watching you climbers ninja up the ice chutes like arctic monkeys."

"Arctic monkeys..." Despite myself, I chuckle.

"How often do you visit the park? I wonder if I've seen you climb and didn't even know it?"

Considering how frequently I go with or without Chuck this time of year, it's a distinct possibility. Especially since I've packed in extra time there this week in anticipation of the storm. Before I think through my logic more carefully, however, I finally let self-pity get the better of me. "You and I both know you'd never forget seeing me at the ice park. I'm the only Freddy Krueger looking guy in the place."

Luna's eyes round, and her mouth drops open into a lovely little O shape that I'd give my grandfather's cabin and all my worldly wealth to kiss. Her eyes narrow, and she turns her head to the side. "That doesn't make any sense. Everyone has to wear helmets at the ice park. It's a rule. Are you trying to test me or something?"

"No, just trying to get the elephant-in-the-room part of our meeting over with."

"Alright then. If you're ready, I'm ready."

The silence is deafening, and I immediately rue opening this Pandora's Box.

"What happened to your face?" she asks calmly, never

taking her eyes off my forward gaze but cutting a careful balance between looking at me and observing my scars unflinchingly.

I give her the answer I give all individuals brave enough to ask, "I lost in a contest with a roadside bomb."

"Where?"

"Afghanistan."

"How long ago?"

"Five years. It ended my career, engagement, social life, and future as I'd always imagined it. Fun times." Her expression remains unreadable despite my unsolicited confession. It's the opposite of the pity I expected to flood her face.

Chapter Eight

LUNA

"What, no pity stare or words?" Ledger asks, a strange fierceness animating his face as if he's preparing for an argument.

"That sucks." I shrug.

"That's all you have to say?" He scrunches his brows together, leaning towards me.

"Life sucks for you. For me. For Naomi and my grandpa. For everyone at some point or another."

"Yeah, but you have to admit this is a lot of suckage for one man."

"It is. But it could also be worse."

"Worse? Do you have an eye problem or something?"

"No, but I've definitely seen worse. So, I'm not quite sure why it seems like you're hiding out from the world. No offense, but that's not much of a contingency plan...especially for a Marine."

"Who are you to speak to me like this? And how do you know anything about being a wounded warrior?"

I frown. "I more or less grew up around them, thanks to my grandpa, who was a double amputee. We went to the VA a

43

lot and visited his friends. Some came by the house, too. So, I got to see the full spectrum of how people dealt with their injuries. Some soldiered on despite horrifying injuries. Far worse than yours. Others gave up for far less...too angry at God, life, whatever to keep trying."

"You sound like you're eighty years old or something. What the heck?"

"I'm twenty-four," I correct.

"How does someone so young talk like they're so old?"

"You're not the first to accuse me of being an old soul. I've seen a lot. What can I say? Since we're sharing personal information, how old are you, Starboy?"

"Are you really going to persist in calling me that?"

I shrug. "Last time I checked, I have nothing better to do."

"I'm thirty-nine."

"Okay."

Cocking his head, he orders, "So, tell me more about how you got so jaded."

"There's nothing to tell," I reply with a shrug. "Grandpa and Grandma raised me because both of my parents were immature deadbeats who never got their acts together. I may not wear my scars as visibly as you do. But believe me, I have them."

"Is that why you don't flinch when you look at me? Because you're used to seeing human wreckage?" As soon as the words leave his mouth, regret clouds his face.

"Human wreckage?" I shake my head. "I don't even know what you're talking about. My grandfather is a good man, and despite spending all of the time I've known him in a wheelchair or trying to get around on prosthetics, he's never let those injuries keep him down or hold him back. The same goes for many of his friends, though not all."

"It's different when it's your face," Ledger grumbles with

more of the same fierceness. As if he needs to believe with every ounce of his being the lie he tells himself.

"Maybe. But all I know is my grandpa would give anything to walk around or run one more time, let alone ice climb..."

Ledger flinches.

"Look, I'm not interested in comparing one man's war injuries to another's. We all have our crosses to bear. Who knows why? And I'll grant you the selection process for life's burdens makes very little sense. But what are any of us going to do about it?"

Silence.

Ledger looks down for a long moment as if he's processing my last statement.

"I don't know how long you have on that pizza crust. But it's smelling pretty darn amazing, and I'm hungry enough to eat a horse after the day I had. So, would you mind if I pull it out, top it, and get it back in the oven?"

To my surprise, the big, brawny man closes his eyes, his Adam's apple working as he swallows hard. When his baby blues flash open again, they're red, and his voice sounds raw as he says quietly, "Thank you." Somehow, I feel like he's saying "thank you" for far more than dressing a pizza, and it makes me long to know him better and to understand the hidden undercurrent of his communication.

Even though I can't read him, tears well in my eyes, and I beeline for the fridge. Kneeling before the bottom shelf, I spend an inordinate amount of time getting blasted by cold air and staring indecisively at his beer collection as I pull myself together.

He finally asks, "Are you striking out on brews? I have more in the garage if you want to take a peek."

I shake my head, discreetly wiping my cheeks. "No, it's just been a long day, and my brain is flat-lining." I grab the first bottle my hand reaches Uncompahgre Pale Ale. "As for pizza toppings, you strike me as a cheese and pepperoni guy. Simple, to the point, but always delicious."

"I hope you're talking about the pizza. Otherwise, you're going to make me blush, Luna."

My cheeks flush, and I stand up, holding bags of cheese, pre-sliced pepperoni, and my beer. I close the fridge door with my hip before setting the toppings on the counter. Then, I twist the cap with the bottom of his hoodie to protect my hand. "Guys like you don't blush. You smolder, right?"

"Hey, wait." He chuckles, much to my shock. "Is that a reference to the *Jumanji* reboot with the Rock and Jack Black?"

"Indeed, it is," I smile, taking a swig from the bottle as I look in his direction. "I love that movie."

"I love both of them, actually. Tough to beat Robin Williams, after all. That said, I must admit the second one's better."

I search the drawer behind him for oven mitts, finding two I can use. Donning the gloves, I say, "You're behind the times, Ice-Climber. There are three movies out now if you include *The Next Level*. Although I still agree with your assessment that the second one's the best."

The brawny Marine moves to the side, allowing me to open the oven door and pull out the first crust.

"It's too bad the blizzard's so nasty outside. We could try streaming the movie. Is the internet back up?"

I pull my phone from my pocket, glancing at it and shaking my head. The wind howls violently outside, punctuating my answer.

"Well, maybe when the storm blows over, we can give it a shot," I reply, making the surly man's eyebrow climb his forehead.

"When that happens, you'll leave, though."

An artless grin captures my mouth. "When the weather

improves, yeah, I'll have to think about getting to Montrose. But I imagine we'll be friends by then. So catching a movie together or returning to visit you won't feel that strange. Right?"

The Marine looks conflicted, blustering, "I don't do public theaters."

"No worries. I meant your place anyway."

He bites his lower lip, trying not to smile. "That could work..."

"If you're not too busy..."

"If I'm not too busy."

I turn my attention to topping the pizza while he flattens the second piece of dough on a new pan before poking it with a fork, sprinkling it with Italian seasoning, and putting it in the oven.

He washes his hands at the sink, side-eyeing me as I finally let my neurotic flag fly. I order the pepperoni slices over the mozzarella in a perfect spiral formation, slightly overlapping the slices like a deck of cards, radiating out from the center to the edges.

"If I didn't know better, I'd think this means something," he remarks in low, growly tones.

"Only when I'm working with mashed potatoes," I counter, drawing another unexpected chuckle from him as he opens the fridge door, pulling out a bottle and opening it.

"*Close Encounters of the Third Kind*. You know your movies, girl."

I shrug. "Grandpa and I watched a lot of films together. Are you freaked out by my neuroses yet? Believe me, this is only the beginning."

He takes a draw from his beer, shaking his head. "I've got my own issues when it comes to compulsions. Maybe not perfectionism like you, or whatever you call this, but certainly painfully meticulous attention to detail."

Ledger stands next to me, and I savor his cologne's spicy, woodsy smell, declaring, "You smell amazing."

"Do I?"

"Yes, you do," I reply, straightening up and leveling my gaze on his face. My cheeks heat because he's a drop-dead gorgeous man despite all he's endured. Maybe even more so because of what he's gone through. He may not realize it, but there's a gravity of strength to him that only comes from great suffering. I wish he could see this about himself. "Now, back to that previous comment about meticulous attention to detail. I imagine it helps with ice climbing."

"That's for sure." He runs his free hand through his brown hair, inadvertently making it stick up in the back. It gives him a bit of that irresistible bedhead look. It also gives me an insatiable need to touch him. Not only because of my neuroticism but because something about the man continues to draw me irresistibly.

That said, my hands are covered in pepperoni oils. *No bueno.* So, I turn to the sink to wash them, calling over my shoulder, "And astronomy?"

He nods.

I dry my fingers on the hand towel on the counter before returning to stand by the moody mountain man, my heart pounding at what I contemplate. Before I hesitate, or he makes things awkward, I stand on my tiptoes, running my hands through the back of his long waves to smooth them. The moment I touch him, he pulls back with a sharp exhale.

"What are you doing?" he hisses, his eyes flashing with an unnameable emotion.

"Sorry, but your hair was ruffled in the back. It was cute and all, but after what you said about meticulous attention to detail, I assumed that meant having nothing out of place, including your hair."

He furrows his brow, his eyes swimming with too many emotions to translate.

I add, "I'm sorry. I should have warned you first or asked for permission. If it makes you feel any better, my day job is as a hairdresser. So, I know what I'm doing."

"I'm just not used to *this*," he says, the muscles bouncing in his jawline as he clenches his teeth and gestures large with his hands.

"I'm sorry if I've made you feel uncomfortable."

"Not you. Just everything about this situation. Your age. Your gender. You touching me. You being in my cabin. You looking at me the way you're looking at me now."

"No offense, but that answer was pretty much all you, you, you..."

"I'm trying," he whispers.

"I'm sorry. I didn't mean to upset you with my presence."

"It's not that." He shakes his head, and his eyes find mine, his face unreadable. "I don't know that 'upset' is the right word, and your presence is good. I really like it. More than I care to admit, honestly. But *this* is all very unexpected."

"For me, too," I say with a bittersweet smile. Only I would find a gorgeous cowboy-mountain-man rescuer with wounds so deep and shields so high a hand in his hair is too much.

My mind spins the dialogue to come with Naomi, where I describe the culmination of my sad love life with an impossibly romantic rescue by a guy I could easily fall for. *If* he could ever get over the rough hand fate dealt him...

Chapter Nine

"**W**e need a change of subject. Tell me about your day, Luna. I want to know everything. Well, at least everything you feel like telling me."

"You know the basic gist of what happened. It was just a lot. Seeing Naomi in pain. Seeing how bad her injuries were. Waiting for the search and rescue guys to get there. Feeling so helpless..."

His Adam's apple bobs as he swallows and nods. "There's nothing worse than seeing someone you care about injured and hurting." His voice sounds raw, haunted by the statement. I know from my grandfather's experiences what bothers him the most about his time in Vietnam are the injured comrades he couldn't help or save.

"Did you see that often?" I ask quietly.

He nods, taking a deep breath. "Once is more than enough. But in Afghanistan, there were a few incidents that come back to me in vivid flashbacks. You should know that I've still got pretty bad PTSD. It can wake me up at night screaming. I hope that won't happen with you here, but just in case you hear anything weird, don't worry about it."

Despite the even tone of his voice, I notice a slight tremor in his hand as he runs it through his hair again. My eyes tick towards his ruffled waves, and he sighs, resigned. "You can smooth it out if it bothers you. Looking at this pizza, it's pretty obvious you like things a certain way."

"Thank you." I lean up towards him, caressing the hair along the back of his head down to his shoulders, our faces coming the closest they've been since the car ride. "You know, I don't mean to be rude, but you could really use a haircut." My fingers linger in his wild mane, assessing his unkempt locks. I hold my breath, marveling at the fact that despite my scrutiny, he doesn't pull away this time. I imagine this is what it must feel like to pet a wild lion.

"Oh, yeah? A haircut? And let me guess. You're the hairdresser for the job?" He arches his eyebrow, his baby blues searing into me.

"I'm really good."

"I don't know," he says morosely, hanging his head, even though my fingers still linger at the back of his muscular neck.

Clearing my throat, I add, "I wasn't going to tell you this because it doesn't really matter. But maybe, under the circumstances, it will help. I sometimes volunteer with the VFW to provide free haircuts to wounded warriors. So, nothing about you or your scars will surprise me."

His face tightens, and silence fills the room for a long stretch, punctuated solely by the violent sounds of the blizzard outside. "I couldn't let you do that. I mean, you're my guest."

"No offense. But do you have many hairdressers lining up to tame your tresses?"

"Tame my tresses?" He chuckles, his voice softening. "Has anybody ever told you that you have a way with words?"

I stare up to the right in thought. "I'm a hairdresser by weekday and a wildlife watercolorist by weekend. So, no."

"Well, let me be the first...along with pointing out you're pretty much as geeky as me."

"Maybe more so. Which qualifies me to point out that..." My fingertips run back and forth through his silky, mahogany locks for emphasis. "Even geeks need haircuts."

"You have a point," he says quietly, turning his beautiful eyes towards me. "I was just hoping to spare you this," he says, motioning towards his left side. "Not drastically alter the way you feel about me. Not that I know how you feel about me, but you get what I mean..."

My right hand comes up to the hair veiling his left side. "May I?" I ask.

His jaw hardens so that I can hear the teeth grinding in his mouth. To my surprise, however, he nods.

Tentatively, I sweep the hair back from his face, staring long and hard at his wounded side. The skin is angry and red, pulled oddly in places and thick and puckered in others. While his nose and lips remain almost untouched, he's missing his left ear save for a small mound of flesh, and his beard ends, except for patchy spots, where the scar tissue begins. The scars run in angry ridges and lumps down his neck, disappearing into his black T-shirt.

"The bathroom's down the hallway if you think you're going to be sick," he says in a caustic voice. His eyes flicker towards the tears running down my cheeks. "No, Luna," he scolds quietly. "Please don't cry because of me."

"I can't help it," I say, biting my lip and fighting hard not to sob.

"It's that bad, huh?"

Sighing, I explain, "Every single one of these marks, these scars bear witness to the pain and violence you endured and overcame. It's hard for me to look at only because it's hard to think about what you went through. But it doesn't change the way I feel about you, and it doesn't make me see you any differently. If anything, it cements my conclusion that you're the most impressive man I've ever met."

His eyes narrow. "Now, I know you're lying."

My right hand hovers over his hurt cheek, and I register the ambivalence in his eyes for a split-second before he pulls away. "I better check on the pizza. The last thing we want is it burned to a crisp." He adds darkly, "No pun intended." I assume it's a reference to his face.

Ledger searches for the oven mitts before opening the door, releasing a flash of hot air. He pulls the perfectly browned pie out of the oven, setting it on the part of the kitchen counter already lined with a couple of folded towels.

Testily, he barks, "Believe me, I've heard every line in the book when it comes to my face, and why I need to count my blessings. Or see the glass as half full instead of half empty. I don't need a pep talk from a total stranger about why everything's okay. Because if everything were okay, you wouldn't weep when you looked at me." His baby blues glare at me for a long, tense moment before he goes back to bustling around the kitchen, putting the second pizza in the oven.

Growing up with my grandpa makes me realize I can do nothing to help this man in his current mood. Instead, I open pantry doors, searching until I find plates. Next, I rifle through drawers until Ledger asks grumpily, "What are you looking for?"

"Your pizza cutter thingie," I say, motioning with my hand.

"Third drawer to the left with the spatulas and wooden spoons."

"Thank you," I reply, working hard to keep my voice calm and unaffected by the exchange moments earlier. Despite my grandpa's make-do personality, living with him was no picnic. His mood could fluctuate wildly between depression, self-pity, and anger. I learned young not to take it personally...or put up with it when he went overboard. I'm ready to draw the same line with Ledger.

We eat our pizzas in silence at the small dining table in the kitchen, sipping beers and listening to the howling of the snowstorm. The air feels thick, the night interminable. The tension in the room merely confirms what I should have figured out hours ago. That the real wounds motivating Ledger to hide from the world have nothing to do with his scars and everything to do with an ugly internal struggle I most likely will never understand...or have any say in.

But as we continue to eat in silence, his glances soften, and the corners of his mouth turn up as though he's offering an olive branch. I can't help but return the smile, unable to hold a grudge against the handsome, grumpy Marine.

"*Moonstruck?*" Ledger's voice slices through my thoughts. He waggles his eyebrow at me, elaborating, "I have it on DVD. Are you a fan of Cher and early Nick Cage?"

"It's one of my all-time favorites," I confess, wiping my mouth with my napkin and allowing my shoulders to relax slightly.

"I don't know about you, but I won't be able to fall asleep anytime soon. Even though I spent the day ice climbing. So, yeah, we might as well be sleepless together...which reminds me, I also have *Sleepless in Seattle*. Do you have a preference?"

I sigh with relief, ready to put the earlier drama behind us and banish the loneliness and unease I feel in this cabin. "Let's watch both."

"Deal," he replies, nodding resolutely. The expression on his face lets me know he's trying, and despite the earlier weirdness, my heart melts at the effort.

"I would have never taken you for a romance movie kind of guy, Ledger," I observe, cocking my head to the side and making no secret of staring at his face, both the good and the bad side. He must be getting more accustomed to this because he doesn't flip his hair or turn his head.

Ledger stands up, grabs his plate, and rounds the table to take mine. "I may not be into all that lovey-dovey stuff in real life. But even a guy like me has a heart."

None of this is news to me. Well, perhaps the part about not being into "lovey-dovey" stuff, but that's also the bit I imagine he's lying about. Especially to himself.

I help the Marine put pizzas away, clean the kitchen, and load dishes. After the place looks spotless and the dishwasher swirls and swishes, Ledger heads to the fridge for another beer. "Can I get you another one, Snoopy?"

"Snoopy?" I ask, raising a quizzical eyebrow.

"Yeah, 'cause you like snooping around my kitchen and life."

I chuckle, feeling my cheeks flush. "Sure. I'll take another of the Pale Ales. And I'm going to choose to see your nickname as a compliment, cowboy."

He flips the switch in the kitchen and turns off all the lights except a night light, which is plugged into the outlet over the stove. It casts a warm glow on the rustic tiles lining the backsplash.

Pointing towards them, I ask, "Where are those tiles from? They look Moroccan or something."

"They're from Greece. See what I mean by snoopy? You're curious about everything. I can't think of a name that suits you better."

"Does that make you Woodstock, then?"

He frowns. "I talk about as much as Woodstock most of the time."

"He was a grumpy little bird, as I recall. I can see the resemblance."

"Yeah, but I'm already starboy, ice-climber, cowboy, probably mountain man. Definitely cowboy-mountain-man, if a nickname can even be that long. I think nicknames should have a three-option limit, four max. Don't you?"

"What's the fun in that?"

He shoots me a frown.

I raise my palms, chuckling. "But it's your house, so it's your rules. Isn't that how it goes?"

"It is. Come on, Snoop. Let's go binge-watch romance movies so your Valentine's Day isn't a total bust. Do you need to call Naomi again? Or check my satellite phone for texts?"

"Oh, yes. Thank you."

After grabbing the phone, he helps me into my jacket, escorting me out into the darkness and whipping wind in search of a signal. Fortunately, his texts load right away, including one telling me Naomi's heading into surgery tomorrow at six in the morning. It says she or her parents will text afterward with an update.

Back inside, he helps me out of my jacket, asking, "What's the word?"

"She's going into surgery first thing in the morning." I look down at my hands, guilt transforming my stomach into a heavy pit. "I still can't believe this happened, and I feel like it's my fault. Naomi wanted to stay in town today to go shopping. But I was the one who insisted on getting in some skiing before the weather changed."

"Everyone in Ouray had the same idea today, Luna. You can't blame yourself for it... Hey, you prayed with her over the phone earlier. Would doing that now make you feel a little better?" His eyes narrow, his face bashful.

I swallow loudly. "Absolutely. Thank you for suggesting it, Ledger."

He shrugs. "Don't get me wrong. I'm no believer or anything, but my best friend, Chuck, is into that stuff. And you seem to be, too, from the half of your earlier conversation that I couldn't avoid overhearing."

I know he heard it, yet I still tease, "You listened in on my conversation?"

His face tenses shyly, and he pauses before explaining, "No offense, Snoop, but you've got cell yell like none other. I think my neighbor, Mrs. Campbell, heard you, and she's, like, five miles that way." He points toward the front door.

Before I can retort properly, he steps forward, towering above me. Grabbing my hands in his, he bows his head toward mine, the motions awkward but not unpracticed. He waits patiently as I find fitting words, painfully aware to the point of distraction of the electricity zinging back and forth between our fingers and palms. By the end, goosebumps trail my hands and forearms, and I shiver with want. *Does he feel it, too?* His face looks stony, but after I release his hands, he reflexively fists and stretches them, making the corners of my mouth turn up.

I follow him into the living room, cuddling up on the sofa facing his flatscreen. I admire his muscular back and shoulders as he kneels before the hearth, stirring the fire and throwing a couple more logs on. Once the blaze roars, he flips through a cabinet filled with DVD jewel cases, making hollow, clicking sounds until he produces *Moonstruck*.

As Dean Martin's deep voice croons *That's Amore*, Ledger disappears down the hallway, returning with a couple of fake fur blankets lined in forest green satin. He throws one unceremoniously in my direction before taking a seat as far from me as possible on the opposite end of the couch.

I feel rejected and swallow hard, trying not to care. But then I notice his heated stare in my direction, and he says softly, "This goes without saying, but Happy Valentine's Day, Snoopy."

Chapter Ten

LEDGER

I wake up with full arms and a fuller heart, deliciously warm and relaxed, with silky tresses tangled in my fingers. Slow breathing fills my ears, warming the spot over my heart as I realize that Luna and I fell asleep together on the couch. And at some point, somehow, despite the distance I put between us, the lovely watercolorist snuggled into me.

In sleepy response, I must've wrapped my arms around her because now I hold her tightly to my chest, feeling the boom of my pulse reverberating against her soft, curvy frame, her head cradled against my chest. Nothing has ever felt more right or torn me more thoroughly apart.

My mind panics, racing for the best way to extricate myself from this situation. I imagine her waking up gently, her eyes narrowing as her body stirs with uncoordinated motions before she gets a long look at my face, shattering the peace of the early morning living room with a frightened gasp or scream. The vision makes my heart sputter and wobble.

Do I really think she'll do this after last night? I don't know. But it's the narrative that makes letting her go the easiest. And I know I must let her go. Because even if she thinks she can be okay with my appearance, even if she's extra brave or self-sacrificing or some kind of a wounded warrior groupie, she hasn't felt the full force and sting of my situation yet.

Luna hasn't had to go out in public, registering the disgusted looks on people's faces as they assess me, their faces shrouded in curiosity and terror. She hasn't seen the pitying glances sure to come her way or heard the incredulity in people's voices when they realize we're together. I could never put her through that kind of nightmare. It's why I called off my engagement after the accident. One look at my fiancée's face after the big reveal, and I knew it was over. Breaking it off quickly was the least mercy I could bestow on her.

My mind twirls and turns, twists and tortures me as my body does something curious. It goes into full revolt, refusing to let go of the beauty in my arms. Despite the alarms going off in my brain, every muscle in my body, every nerve fiber, every cell clings fiercely to her and this moment. I savor this stolen intimacy with all five senses, straining to remember it with perfect clarity for a lifetime.

Ignoring the downward spiral of my tangled thoughts, I close my eyes and clutch her desperately, trying to commit this experience to memory forever. The faint smell of her lavender and rose fragrance, the electricity of her touch, even in sleep. The intense sense of comfort and security she instills, something I didn't know I needed but thirst for to the depths of my soul.

I want Luna Solace. I yearn for her more than any woman I've ever known. And I long for the impossible future she represents and the way her love could piece me back together. Make me a whole man again, at least below the surface. This desire goes beyond reason and logic. It makes no sense. It just aches and thirsts and demands...to the very roots of my soul. How will I ever satisfy the intensity of this hunger, strong enough to break what's left of me in bits like a ship against coastal rocks?

The cold lump in the center of my chest warms and expands, and my heart beats back to life, thrilling and terrifying me. My throat tightens, a knot forming, and the backs of my eyes sting. Hot, wet trails follow, covering my cheeks, and I pray to God she doesn't wake up and see me like this...so utterly vulnerable. But I can't free the arms holding her to wipe away the tears without ruining this moment. And I refuse to do that, savoring every sensation as though it were my last.

I don't know how much time passes, but my senses slowly return to me. Outside the shell of warmth beneath the blankets on the couch, the air feels inordinately frosty. My eyes scan the room carefully, noting the lifeless DVD player and other electronic device interfaces. The storm must've knocked out power.

No wonder Luna cuddled with me. My damp, exposed cheeks provide all the evidence I need. It's freezing in here. But why hasn't the generator gone on? I blink hard several times, straining my ears for its telltale growl. Nope. Nothing.

"What's wrong?" A sweet, feminine voice croons from the crook of my arms. I stiffen, uncertain how to respond.

A petal-soft hand strokes my cheek, palming my face as her thumb runs back and forth over my beard, making scratchy noises. The most delectable sparks shoot from her fingertips down my neck into the juncture of my heart. The tenderness of her caress and the softness of her words shock and overwhelm me.

Out of all the responses she could have for me this morning, I never allowed myself to contemplate this one. Despite my self-loathing and fear of having others see, touch, or judge my scars, I remain riveted to the couch, swallowing hard as her tiny fingers knit little pieces of me back together with each caress.

"Good morning, Angel," I say warmly, the corners of my mouth turning up despite myself.

She beams at me in response, flooding me with addictive waves of love. "Angel?"

"Yeah." I grin, looking up at the ceiling bashfully before directing the full warmth of my searing gaze on her. Luna's cheeks darken, her nostrils flair, and her eyes dilate, making breathing impossible. I confess, "That's technically my first nickname for you. Which means I get two more..."

She nods, smiling back at me.

Still drowsy enough to speak without a filter, I say, "You know, you shouldn't be allowed to wake up this beautiful. It's pretty much criminal."

"And you shouldn't be such a good liar before daybreak," she replies, running the backs of her fingers over my beard, leaving trails of fire and longing everywhere they fall.

I swallow loudly, fighting the renewed sting at the back of my eyes as I say in a raw voice, "I'm not lying. You're so stunning it hurts me to look at you." Usually, I'd wince if a cheesy line like that crossed my lips. But the tremble of my voice communicates my sincerity.

Her cheeks glow as her tear-filled eyes drink me in, the tension in the room so dense I gasp for relief.

I need a change of subject. "Did you sleep, okay?" I manage, desperate to get a hold of myself.

"I don't think I've ever slept so well on a shared couch." She stirs, stretching in my arms, and disappointment fills me. I'm not ready to let go of her, though I know I should. Yet, to my surprise, she snuggles closer, bringing her hand from my face to my chest.

"I hope I didn't wake you in the middle of the night screaming or talking or anything like that?"

She shakes her head. "No. I think we both slept like babies." Suddenly, guilt floods her face, and she sits up stiffly. "Do you know what time it is? Do you think Naomi's out of surgery yet?"

"I don't know," I say reluctantly, letting go of her and sitting up straighter. I stretch the muscles in my shoulders and neck the best I can without actually relinquishing my place next to this sleeping beauty. Her warmth and tenderness feel like lifelines to me. "The power went off at some point in the night, and the generator didn't turn on. I don't know why."

Luna lets the blankets sag, continuing to move around, and the interior air's uncustomary chill needles me to get up and get busy. If I don't sort things out quickly with the generator, I could end up with frozen pipes and later house flooding.

In the morning's darkness, however, the spell she's woven around me is palpable, inescapable. I need more of her. I bring my hand to Luna's cheek, pushing a stray hair off her face. "I want to remember you like this forever. Is that a creepy thing to admit? Be honest."

She bites her lower lip, her cheeks flushing as her eyes drop to my mouth. "It's not creepy at all." A bittersweet smile captures her soft, kissable lips as she draws closer, covering the gulf between us before I can pull away. Her lips feather over mine, catching me so off guard I freeze. I need to stop her...to back away. But with every throb of my heart, I lose another sliver of reason to her magnetic pull.

Her arms circle my neck, declaring her desire, and I can't deny her. Surrendering to the taste of this alluring woman, I lean in, letting my lips confess my craving. God help me. Luna presses against me, covering my warm, tentative lips with her passionate ones and wresting a needy moan from deep within my chest. Heat floods my core, and my heart smashes around wildly.

I pull back, dangling painfully from the tatters of my shattered willpower, bringing my forehead to rest against hers. I press my eyes shut, confessing breathlessly, "The thought of leaving you right now feels impossible, Angel. But I've got to figure out what's going on with the generator, and I've got to check in on some of my elderly neighbors. And we need to figure out what time it is and get you on the phone with Naomi or the hospital for an update."

I brush my lips over her forehead, and she gives me a disappointed little nod. Before I can stop her, she grabs my cheek again, pulling me towards her for another kiss.

My beautiful little guest doesn't realize the fire she's playing with as a deep warning growl resonates from my chest. My hands glide from her hair down the smooth skin of her neck.

They rest on her delicate shoulders, my thumbs possessively stroking her smooth throat until I draw a whimper from her. Roving over her shoulders, down the contour of her shapely back, they settle at her waist. I cinch her against me, desire knotting thickly in my throat as my thirst for her swallows me whole, deluging me in sensual waves of longing.

I yearn to feel every inch of her pinned against every inch of me, desperate for her touch. A visceral part of me wants to greedily gobble her up, refusing to let her leave me. And I get the strong impression she might be okay with that. But would it be the right thing to do?

I pull back, gasping for air and resting my face in the crook of her neck. My whole body tightens around her as I fight for self-control, letting out a frustrated sigh. Feeling a new fire born at the back of my neck, where her fingers slide through my hair, longing simmers near the boiling point.

"I can't do this," I hiss against her décolletage, pressing my lips against the delicate sweep of her collarbone. Her hands slip beneath my shirt, spreading sizzling flames as she massages and caresses my back. My tongue swipes over her skin, tasting her shoulders. To my satisfaction, she trembles and sighs, urging me on.

Yet, somewhere through the heady haze, a strand of reason lingers, pulled taut like a piano string, sounding in the morning stillness. Drawing back from her neck, I whisper against the shell of her ear, my voice shivering with restraint. "I can't. Please. We have to stop."

"Why?" She exhales sharply.

Desire twists into anger. It's the only way I can do what I know I must...

What does she want from me? Why is Luna doing this?

"We both know you deserve better." I gasp, searching for words, trying to find a way to stop this before it gets any more out of control. I know myself, and I'll never be able to part with her if things progress any further. "Is this a pity thing?" I accuse, pulling back as the sting of my words smacks into her.

"A pity thing?" Her voice trembles, and her brows furrow.

"Yeah, a pity thing. I think it's a fair enough question. I mean, look at me! How could you possibly be attracted to this?" I gesticulate wildly toward my face, channeling every ounce of pent-up love and lust into a volatile explosion of searing anger. Surrendering to fury instead of the tears that threaten to cover my cheeks.

Luna sits back, her eyes rounding and filling with shock. She puts a hand over her mouth as more tears fill her eyes, and I feel like the biggest jerk to ever live. It's more proof that she can do better, that she has to do better than me because I'm no good for her.

Bursting to my feet, I pace back and forth, the ferocious injustice of my life gripping me. *God, why do this to me? And then put this amazing, beautiful, caring angel in my path? What kind of sick joke is this?*

"I have to go," I growl, striding into the kitchen to grab

my satellite phone. I toss it gently on the couch next to Luna because I can't risk getting too close to her again. She's an impulse I can't control.

Tears slide down her cheeks, her visage pale and stunned. My arms ache to hold her and comfort, but I'm the reason for her pain. My heart drops into my stomach. *Nice job, Ledger.*

Running my hand through my hair, I say, "I'll be back later." Stomping towards the coat rack, I stop short, staring at the dead hearth. "Let me build the fire back up for you first."

I don't leave until flames glow bright, warm, and mesmerizing. My eyes flicker to Luna, jealous of how the golden firelight licks over the parts of her my hands and lips caressed less than an hour ago. Swallowing hard, I head for the door. I can't let whatever this is between us go on any further.

Chapter Eleven

LUNA

I don't know how long I stare shellshocked at the fire once Ledger leaves. But it's a relief to get away from the frantic swirl of his emotions because they mirror my own tangled feelings.

He's a deeply wounded and traumatized man, and I knew this from nearly the moment I met him. The way he repeatedly turned to the side, hiding half of himself from me. How he simultaneously welcomed me into his cabin while pulling back at every turn.

My mind flies in reverse through time, indulging in the delicious feeling of his fingers in my hair, the tenderness flooding his eyes, the softness and warmth of his skilled lips moving over mine. His nickname for me...

He tried as hard as he could...until he couldn't try anymore. I shouldn't have pushed him, but I couldn't help myself. Because I want him in a way I've never wanted any man. And the urgency of knowing I have to leave only compounds my impatience.

Waking up in his arms, wrapped in his masculine strength and warmth, smelling his musky, foresty scent and staring into his clear blue eyes cemented it for me. Everything feels so right when we're together...for those brief moments when Ledger's walls come down.

I can't leave without him knowing how I feel. But how do I communicate a reality he seems determined to deny?

Suddenly, light floods the cabin, and I hear the heater come on, indicating the return of electricity. I putter around, turning off unnecessary lights and adding wood to the fire, staring long and hard at the cowboy-mountain-man's pre-injury photos. Heading into the guest bedroom, I retrieve my portable watercolor kit, knowing what I have to do.

Carefully, I remove the memory box from the wall, setting it next to me at the kitchen table while I work, starting with pencils and then filling in with vibrant shades of black, brown, and various hues of tan and a little cobalt blue.

By the time I hear him trudge up the porch stairs, darkness shrouds the cabin windows, and I've drawn the curtains. Numerous logs have gone onto the fire, the memory box is back on the wall, and I've snacked on cold pizza and sipped on green tea I found in one of his kitchen cabinets. My watercolor kit is packed in my backpack once more, and I've laundered my clothes and showered in preparation for tomorrow and the potential break in the weather...

The break that may see me to Montrose...and away from Ledger forever. My heart aches at the thought, but I can't make him pursue what he doesn't think he deserves, no matter what I say or how hard I try.

The cowboy looks across the room at me with palpable longing, fueling the fire incinerating me. But I remind myself there's a world of difference between emotions and actions. He clears his throat, his face tight, and his voice restrained. "What's the latest on Naomi?"

"I've talked with her parents on and off throughout the day, and this evening, I spoke to Naomi, too, which is a huge relief. She sounded groggy, a side-effect of the anesthesia and heavy-duty pain medications she's on, and her parents say she now has at least eight screws in her ankle and two plates to stabilize a broken tibia, fractured fibula, and dislocated ankle."

Ledger winces. He removes his coat, hangs it on the rack, and bends down to remove his snow boots. "We need to get you to her."

"Yes."

He lets out a long exhale as he turns his back towards me. "The weather broke about an hour ago, and the forecast is clear through tomorrow night. So, I'll get up at dawn and clear the driveway with the tractor. Then, we'll see about getting your car out of the ditch and if it's drivable. Either way, I'll get you to Montrose."

"Thank you."

He continues to stand with his back to me, saying nothing.

Swallowing hard, I finally pierce the silence. "How was everything outside?"

He turns, his shoulders hunched and his head angled down so that his hair drapes around his face again. "The cattle, hens, and goats were all good. The barn's toasty warm and dry. And Mrs. Campbell is okay. Two winters back, I found her after she broke her hip and had to call the ambulance and clear a pathway for them to reach her place. So, I worry about her the most."

"I'm glad she's okay. How many cows do you have?" I ask as he passes by me. The inconsequential question does the trick, making him stop and look at me again. He lets out another lengthy sigh, his blue eyes guarded. "Fifty head thereabouts."

"So, you really are a cowboy?"

His face remains impassive. "Yes, ma'am."

Ma'am. After this morning, is that really where we're at?

68

Ma'am? No word has ever pierced me so thoroughly, but I remind myself where impatience got me this morning.

He says stiffly, "Look, I need a shower. After that, are you good with more pizza and beer?"

I nod, fighting hard against the tears welling in the backs of my eyes.

"Good. And then, I'd like to show you something before you leave me."

Before I leave him? More like before he pushes me away... I open my mouth to speak, but the large, muscular man's already halfway down the hallway, disappearing with a couple more strides.

An hour later, we eat reheated pizza and drink our beers silently. The suffocating quiet accompanies us as we clean up the kitchen, and the sounds of dishes, silverware, and rinsing water fragment the thick tension as we load the washer. Curiously, he brews a pot of coffee before filling a thermos and topping it off with cream. I stare raptly at this process, confused by what's next when he muddies the waters even more. "You ready to see my first love?"

I raise my eyebrows, confused by his question. "Okay."

Ledger heads down the hallway towards his bedroom door, and my pulse pounds. I follow him into the neat room with its California king awash in fluffy white duvets and plaid blankets. He motions me towards a funny little door that looks like it's for a closet, opening it and inviting me to pass through. Behind me, he grabs a couple of blankets, still clutching the thermos, and explains, "We're headed back outside, so you'll want to stay bundled up for this."

He opens the door, and a wooden staircase greets us, wrapping around a tower reminiscent of climbing a lighthouse. At the top, he flips some switches, and red lights lining the floor and the walls illuminate revealing a modest-sized room. The lights provide enough light to keep from stumbling without needing my eyes to adjust from darkness to light.

Overhead, a dome looms. He presses a few buttons, and it slides open, causing a strangled hiss to leave my throat as I greedily devour panoramic views of the night sky. The Milky Way glitters and glows, brightly and more stunning than I've ever seen it, the astronomical bodies in the sky more numerous than the grains of sand on a beach.

As my eyes adjust, I make out a massive telescope in the center of the room and an adjoining space that resembles a study. Bookshelves line the walls, and a large desk half covered in charts houses a computer tower with two massive monitors.

"What do you think?"

"It's amazing!" I reply breathlessly, aware of the total inadequacy of my words. Tears fill my eyes as I try to absorb the thousands upon thousands of objects glowing in the night sky, all too easily forgotten in the haze, fog, and light pollution of a Bay Area night. "This reminds me of Great Basin National Park," I say, wrapping my arms around myself as I look up, drinking in the cosmic views. The chill of the night air hits me, raising goosebumps on my flesh.

Ledger comes up behind me with a blanket, wrapping it around my shoulders and pulling me into his arms. "I'm sorry." His voice sounds raw, and he nestles his face against the hair at the nape of my neck, breathing hard.

I lean back into his warmth and strength as he pulls the hair back from my neck, showering me in tiny, tender kisses. My heart beats so loudly I'm certain he can hear it.

"I would give anything to be the man you need, Angel. But I can't..." His voice breaks at the end, and the kisses transform into hot tears as his chest shakes slightly behind me.

My bottom lip trembles, and my face scrunches as I try to hold it together. Hanging onto his hands and sniffling, I work hard to steel my voice, pausing for a long time before I manage, "I don't agree."

"You don't have to for me to be right."

"But you aren't right..."

"I don't want to argue with you," Ledger replies gruffly.

"And I don't want to argue with you..." I bring my hand up to his cheek, stroking his moist beard gently. The finality of my upcoming departure grips me, and I mourn the loss of what will never be.

I never got to cut his hair or see him ice-climbing. We never finished watching *Sleepless in Seattle* together. And I have yet to figure out why the universe knit us so tightly together...only for it to end this way.

Darkness closes in cold and oppressive around us as my eyes focus on the distant twinkling stars, piercing centuries of void with sheer, white light. "Have you ever been to Great Basin?" I whisper.

"No."

"It has stunning night skies. It's one of my favorite national parks for nighttime viewing."

"Is it? I'll have to check it out." He whispers the words as his lips graze over my collarbone again, and his fingers thread into my hair, caressing my tresses. I close my eyes, reveling in his sensual touch.

"I love it. I spent last spring living and working in Baker, and I'm trying for an artist-in-residency post there this coming summer."

"That's an impressive goal, Luna."

"Well, we'll see what happens..."

Pressing his lips against the shell of my ear, he says quietly, "I may not know you that well yet, but I do know you're the kind of woman who gets what she puts her mind to. So, I'd wager Great Basin is on your horizon for summer."

"Would you meet me there?"

"We'll see." He shrugs. "National parks are tough for me, you know. Lots of people..."

I nod, trying to ignore my sinking heart. Silence engulfs us again as Ledger's reality finally hits me. Outside of a trusted handful of people in Ouray, he really is hiding from life.

"So, why is this your first love?" I ask, turning my head slightly to snuggle against his face, feeling the smoothness of his wounded cheek against mine. I stiffen, wondering if this is a miscalculation. Closing my eyes tightly, I wait for his anger to hit me. Instead, he holds me patiently, letting me touch his most vulnerable side. Despite the innocence of the interaction, I have never experienced greater intimacy as he gives me access to the parts of himself he hides from the entire world.

Ledger's deep voice breaks the silence. "My grandpa used to bring me up here to his little makeshift observatory to scope out the stars and record what we saw. It looked a lot different back then because I've done a lot of upgrades. But he introduced me to chasing comets, observing planets, and dreaming of bigger and better ways to map out and learn about our galaxy. Which is where this thing comes in handy," he says, nodding towards the telescope in the middle of the room. "I'm an astronomical observer, and I teach remote classes at the University of Boulder in astronomy. I've also spent the last couple of years working with some postdoctoral students on a new computer model to generate the most accurate maps of our galaxy to date. In the process, I've identified and named a handful of stars and comets."

"You do all of this?" I ask, arching my eyebrows. Suddenly, I feel small and intimidated. After all, I'm just a hairdresser with art ambitions on the side.

"Yes, I was an astronomy major before I was a Marine. Are you ready to do some nighttime observing with me, Snoop?"

"I would love to," I reply quietly. His arms loosen around me, and I rue the loneliness that engulfs me. But I also welcome the change of pace, no longer wanting to focus on the bittersweetness of our coming goodbye.

Chapter Twelve

LEDGER

L una and I spend the night exploring the show in the heavens. The clearness of the bone-cold darkness makes scoping out the sky's most impressive constellations, planets, and stars possible. By the time she grows drowsy and her breathing soft and relaxed under the heap of blankets on the observatory floor, I can barely keep my eyes open. Closing the dome is the last thing I remember.

A few hours later, I awaken with a start to vibrating in my pocket. I lie on the floor next to my sleeping guest, my arms wrapped tightly around her. My left arm is numb, pinned beneath her sleeping body, and it takes me a moment to retrieve my phone, realizing the vibration comes from the alarm I set.

That's right. I have a pre-dawn date with the tractor. Talk about lousy planning, especially when I could stay here, warm and snuggled against my dream girl.

Hitting the snooze button for fifteen more minutes, I snuggle back into my drowsy companion, desperate to remember the feel of her soft body forever. I don't know how I'll let her go. Or try to live without her.

Inner turmoil guts me as a thousand selfish possibilities play out in my mind, alluring and compelling but wrong. Completely wrong. Luna deserves better, and I will be the man to give it to her, my last and greatest display of selfless love. One I fear she'll never understand, which breeds a bitter-sweet anguish.

All too soon, the phone vibrates again. This time, I fall back on my military discipline and training, stirring gently so that the woman in my arms can sleep while I work.

Kissing her cheek, I stare at her long and hard, whispering, "I love you, Luna Solace, and I always will."

The frigid air of the darkened morning revitalizes me, fortifying my determination to do the right thing by the stunning woman nestled upstairs in the observatory. She deserves the best of everything this world has to offer. And that includes a man she doesn't have to feel ashamed of the world knowing about or seeing.

I may be cursed infinitely to this half-life existence, but she doesn't have to be. And no matter how sweet, loving, or self-sacrificing her natural tendencies are, I can't let her ruin her life with me.

❧

After clearing my driveway and feeding her breakfast, I load Luna's belongings into my Jeep. Slowly, we make our way to where she left her vehicle. It takes about fifteen minutes to locate, thanks to deep snow, but once I do, I use the winch on the front of my Jeep to pull her car from the ditch.

After examining it carefully for damage and drivability, I say, "Fortunately, you got off lucky without any damage." She nods, looking down at her feet. "And the weather's cleared enough to get you to Montrose before the next storm this evening."

She continues looking down, her shoulders hunched. Every part of my being longs to draw her into my arms and hold her, declare my feelings for her and greedily claim her as my own. But I love her too much to resign her to my fate.

"Have you ever felt like meeting someone changed the whole trajectory of your life?" she whispers almost inaudibly.

My chest aches at her words, and I nod, looking away, too dangerously close to tears to answer because I refuse to change her whole life. No matter what. She's too young, beautiful, and talented to let me monopolize her future.

Clearing my throat and swallowing hard, I grumble, "Let me get your snow chains on before you run out of time."

She looks away with a sharp sigh, walking back toward my Jeep and getting inside. I have it running with the air blowing expressly for this purpose.

I install chains I find in the trunk of her vehicle, forcing myself to remain resolute. But every move I make feels distant, out-of-body, and surreal. A voice in my head chides me for my stupidity, warning me about the floods of regret to come. I don't know another way to make her happy, and I need her to be happy more than I need to breathe. Not just for today but for the rest of her life.

I pack her vehicle, urging her to stay warm in the Jeep, putting extra pizza, snacks, and drinks for the road in the passenger seat where she can easily reach them. I also place a small box of Valentine's Sweethearts candies with saccharine messages near the food stash. Chuck gave then to me after ice climbing as a gag gift. I never thought I'd find a recipient for them, let alone use them to inadequately express my deep need for the woman I'm letting go. Then, I order her to follow the Jeep down to Ouray and the road out of town, which traffic reports confirm is clear.

We stop in the parking lot of the Visitor's Center by the hot springs, and I realize I can no longer put off the inevitable.

My heart feels ripped from my chest as I look at her now, trying to put all I feel for her into my gaze.

"Thank you for saving me from freezing to death in a blizzard," the brunette beauty says, her mahogany eyes welling with tears even as she works hard to smile.

I step forward, palming her warm, pink cheeks tenderly. "Actually, you're the one who saved me. Don't ever forget it." Tears spill over her lower eyelashes, and I wish everything about this situation were different.

She swallows hard. "Can I call or text you sometime? I don't even have your satellite phone...although Naomi does."

I shake my head, dropping my hand from her cheek and looking down. "It's better to leave things the way they are. But I wish you and Naomi the best."

She frowns, looking away. "Why do you have to be this way?"

"What way?"

"So stubborn..."

"What do you mean?"

She ventures, still looking away, "I'm waiting for you to say what people always say during goodbyes. Whether or not they mean it."

"And what's that?" I ask, rubbing the place over my heart.

"If you're ever in Ouray, look me up..."

I grimace, trying not to make this any more painful than it needs to be. Luna has to move on without any delusions about a guy like me. I erased Naomi's number from my satellite phone this morning for this very reason. Once the loneliness sets back in, I'm afraid I'll be too tempted to reach out to her again, keeping her from moving on. I have to be firm and unyielding about this. Still, I can't deny the beauty before me, so I say begrudgingly, "That goes without saying."

"Alright then. Hey, maybe I'll see you in Great Basin

National Park this summer?" She turns to face me again, her cheeks moist and her eyes red.

"You never know." I nod. I can't help myself as I lean down one more time, grabbing the flaps of her coat's collar and drawing her towards me for a kiss. My lips linger over hers for a long time, savoring her sweet taste and tender warmth. I sweep into her mouth with my tongue, claiming her with some of the pent-up passion driving me insane, and her body melts against me.

An approaching snowmobile motor pulls me back to reality, and I step back breathlessly. Anger flashes inside me at the poor timing.

"Ledger, is that you?" A man yells, and I instantly recognize Chuck's voice. I managed to catch him heading from town back to his place a couple of blocks down the road. Talk about poor timing.

"Yep, it's me, Chuck," I shrug, feeling as busted as a teen in a parked car. He'll be blowing up my cell phone before I know it, looking for an explanation for what he witnessed. But I barely care, waving him off as I relish my final moments with Luna.

Luna raises a questioning eyebrow.

I explain, "That's my ice-climbing buddy and best friend, Chuck." Palming her flushed cheek and taking one last look, I try to commit everything about her to memory. "Drive carefully, Snoop. The roads are going to be icy."

Her eyes beg me for things I can't give her. I have to go. Without hesitation, I turn away, striding to my Jeep, jumping inside, and driving away. I don't look in the rearview mirror because I'm at the end of my willpower's tether, already contemplating going back to claim her.

On the drive home, the isolation of my former life barely has a chance to crash back down around me before my cell phone starts vibrating. Chuck. I ignore the first two calls, but by the third one, I know I have to say something if I'm ever going to get the guy off my back. I reluctantly pick up. "Yep."

"Sorry to rudely interrupt you and your lady friend," he apologizes with thinly veiled curiosity in his voice.

"It's fine. We were saying goodbye."

Silence.

Finally, Chuck asks, "Umm...are you going to fill me in on what's going on? And who Ms. Gorgeous is?"

Even though Chuck's my closest friend and a happily married man, jealousy tackles me. "And why would I do that?"

"Because it's customary for friends to confide in one another, and as I remember, I've told you more than you probably have ever wanted to know about my personal life."

I nod, though my friend can't see me.

What greater harm can any of this do? It's not like I'm ever going to see Luna again. But she'll always be an integral part of my life experience and one I still have to process. So, I do something unthinkable. Maybe all the years of therapy have finally gotten to me. I put my cell phone on my Jeep's Bluetooth device so I can drive and talk hands-free, confessing everything.

I'm still on the phone by the time I reach my driveway.

Chuck's voice sounds exasperated as he asks, "So, you're telling me you finally found a woman you're interested in, and she's obviously into you, and you didn't even get her number? What the heck, Ledger."

"It's for the best," I grumble, entering my cabin and looking around the sad, quiet space. Every place my eyes glance, a memory of Luna greets me. I see her in the kitchen, arranging pepperoni slices on pies like a mosaic maker. Her face greets me from the fridge as she kneels, looking for a cold one. Both of us lie wrapped beneath the blankets on the couch, falling in love with each other in the still of the early morning.

"You're an idiot," he says flatly.

"I'm an idiot, I'm ugly, and I'm lonely. What's new?"

"Seriously, Ledger. God delivered you something precious and special...something to cherish, and you rejected it? What's your problem, man?"

"It would've never worked out," I growl, feeling far worse than Chuck could ever make me, already drowning to the depths of my soul in regret. "It was the only decent thing to do if I really claim to love her."

"So you say..."

I sigh, my eyes falling to a white folded sheet of paper on the kitchen counter. My throat knots as I walk over, retrieving and opening it. I stare at a watercolor portrait of me, one half of my face shrouded in darkness and hair, but the likeness startlingly accurate. Turning it over, I read the words scrolled on the back in pencil: "A man worthy of love..."

I swallow loudly, my chest constricting.

"Ledger, are you still there?" Chuck hollers.

"Yeah, I am. Hold on a sec." After taking a couple of deep breaths to pull myself together, I explain to Chuck what I hold in my hand, feeling like the biggest fool to inhabit the planet. "What does this even mean? I know the conversations we've had about God over the years. Why is He doing this to me? It was hard enough to go through all the pain and horror of acclimating to this future. Why rub salt in the wound?"

"Everyone deserves love."

"Not me. Not with the hand I've been dealt. It's curse enough for me. I can't put this on someone else, too." Guilt seizes me in its steel grip. Guilt for surviving when my comrades died. Guilt for wasting the second chance I've been given because of self-pity. Guilt for wanting things I can't have, even at the expense of others...because my having Luna would come at the expense of her future.

"I think you're being a stubborn idiot right now. Especially over stuff that's ultimately so superficial. But here's the advice I'd give to anyone who felt unloveable. Don't let her go. Figure out how to deserve her."

"Easier said than done..."

He's quiet for a long moment. "As long as you stay mired in self-pity and self-loathing, I agree with you."

Silence.

"You're a former Marine and Pacific Coast surfer. You ice and rock climb. You horseback ride for weeks at a time in the backcountry on cattle drives and jump out of planes for fun. None of these activities leave room for giving up or giving in. You've got to bring that same energy to this situation."

"It's not the same thing. I can't become her burden..."

"So, you'll curse her to be as miserable as you are? From what you've told me, she digs you just as hard. And she put herself out there for you even more, if I understand everything you told me correctly. By making this decision for the both of you, without consulting her, you're denying her love and a future, too."

I sigh, thoughts of the past couple of days pressing in on me, making me miserably lonely without her. My mind spirals, and I can't find the right words to articulate my feelings.

"Are you still there, Ledger?" Chuck asks.

"Yeah," I say tensely.

Silence.

I have to hand it to Chuck for his patience with me over the years, and his forbearance now as I process everything that happened this morning.

Eventually, I ask, "What the heck have I done? I can't believe I let her go like that...without even getting her phone number. What was I thinking?"

"I don't pretend to know what you're thinking right now,

Ledger. Maybe you could try calling the hospital in Montrose to see if they'd relay a message to her through Naomi?"

"I don't even know Naomi's last name," I sigh. "Or when she's discharging. Now that her parents are there, and she's had surgery, I can't imagine they'll keep her much longer."

"Luna must've told you where she lives or given you another way to track her down. You two looked pretty close when I saw you earlier."

"No," I groan frustrated. "What was I thinking? Naomi has my satellite phone number, but I erased hers. And I told Luna not to call or text me."

"Wow, you really were going for finality."

"Yes, I was. Because I thought it was the right thing to do. Maybe it is. I don't know." My voice fades off as I stare at the watercolor again. After another long pause, I say, "Chuck, I think I need to pray. Will you help me?"

"Of course."

Closing my eyes, my heart fills to bursting as I say, "Lord, Dad, God, whatever it is you go by... You sent an angel my way. Like a drop-dead gorgeous, perfect angel, and I messed things up. Big time. But I know you're all about forgiveness and humility...and if you could help me figure out how to deserve her. Well, truthfully, I'll do anything you ask of me..." Tears streak my cheeks, and my voice goes all wonky. Chuck takes over.

But in the stillness of the moment and the desperation of my solitude, a strange peace envelopes me. Like nothing I've felt before. As Chuck goes over all the things church people say, filling in the many gaps and holes in my earlier plea, an overwhelming tranquility settles on me, reassuring me that everything will somehow work out.

SEVEN MONTHS LATER

"What are you doing up here?" the inquisitive, blond boy asks me, carefully picking his way toward me across the boulder field at the base of Wheeler Peak. His mother stands a little ways away on the trail, carrying her backpack and watching our conversation intently.

"I'm an artist-in-residence at Great Basin, working on a watercolor right now."

The dark blonde mother shades her eyes with her hand, watching and listening. She calls to me, "I thought that was a palette and paints you were carrying in the metal case. What's your name? So that I can say I know somebody famous."

I chuckle. "I'm not going for fame or anything, but I have a website and an Instagram account. Luna Solace on both."

"That's a very unique name," she replies with a smile. "I should know because my name's Portia. And this is my son, Gregory. Are you enjoying your artist-in-residency here?"

"Yes, very much. This is hands-down my favorite national park."

"Ours, too," the little boy pipes up, his hazel eyes snapping toward my easel and half-finished painting.

"Did you enjoy the Bristlecone pine grove?" I ask, nodding towards the gnarled collection of wood and green below us. "Some specimens are many thousands of years old."

The boy nods enthusiastically.

"It's always amazing," the woman adds.

Gregory looks over his shoulder at his mother before bragging, "I'm getting my Junior Ranger badge today, and it's my birthday, September 22nd."

"Very nice!" I glance at my half-finished watercolor, frowning. "The autumn equinox. That's a cool birthday to have. How old are you, Gregory?"

"Ten."

"Double digits. That's pretty grown-up. How exciting!"

He puffs his chest with pride, making me laugh.

Portia laughs, too. "Are you going to the stargazing event tonight?"

"Yes, I am. Are you?"

"Yes, Gregory's obsessed with the stars."

I stare at the curious kid, a sudden sadness gripping me. Is this what Ledger was like as a boy? "That's so cool. A future astronomer! Well, maybe I'll see you two tonight."

"Yes, we'll look for you." The woman waves for her son to get back on the trail, and he scrambles like a mountain goat over the boulders as I hold my breath. Despite his agility, painful memories of my last cross-country skiing trip with Naomi wash over me.

"It's the first day of fall, Ledger, and you never showed up," I whisper to myself. It's not like he said he would. But it didn't stop me from waiting breathlessly every summer night of the dark sky programs, scrutinizing tall, dark male forms, listening for familiar deep voices, and reliving painful disappointment again and again.

By early afternoon, the wind picks up, ice-chilled as it glides off the glacier, and I pack up. I have a lot to do before the program tonight, including a hot shower, a quick nap, and a call to my grandparents. I make my way down carefully. The five-mile hike covers an elevation change of more than one thousand feet, which means some fairly steep patches. I navigate the most challenging spots slowly and deliberately.

Since Naomi, I no longer take ankles for granted. Fortunately, she's healed up and back to normal life, with only a scar to show for her ordeal. She spent the summer volunteering at the Monterey Bay Aquarium, using a knee scooter until physical therapy helped her walk again. I make a mental note to text her later for details about her latest man crush, the hunky physical therapist she sees twice a week. I live vicariously through her in the romance department these days.

As the sun sets, I drive towards the Lehman Caves Visitor Center, with its single-story brown facade and wraparound porch on a prominence overlooking the parking lot. The Rhodes Cabin and Great Basin Astronomy Amphitheater sit on the right-hand side facing it. Rugged stone staircases lead to the center, and vast views of the park provide a stunning backdrop.

I savor the breathtaking swatches of vibrant color that declare nightfall. Extravagant shades of hot pink and lavender, splashy layers of periwinkle and gold, juxtaposed against the magnificence is Wheeler Peak, still lightly snow-capped despite the lateness of the season. I have to stop for photos, though I already have hundreds of this mountain.

Twilight settles, and red lights illuminate the parking lot, stairs, and the long walkway to the amphitheater, guiding tourists toward the upcoming event. I high-five some of the younger rangers who I've gotten to know before reporting for duty to my supervisor, Jessica.

"Luna, you're covering the parking lot again tonight. Sound good?"

"Sure thing, boss. Can I assume that means I won't be saying any opening words about the artist-in-residence program, then?" I ask as I don the reflective vest she hands me.

"Nope," she says cheerily. "It's all astronomy tonight."

"Sounds good." After she leaves, I approach cars that roll up the long roadway to the visitors center, leaving behind oceans of sage for the evergreens and scrub brush of the foothills. Directing them where to park, I explain the reason for the red lights, caution them against using their cell phone flashlights that impair night vision, and mention tripping hazards as they head to the amphitheater.

Thirty minutes in, a brown Jeep rolls up, and my mind flashes to Ledger for the briefest of moments. But it's not his vehicle, and it's autumn. I need to move on. The windows roll down, revealing Portia and Gregory.

"Hey, you two!" I greet. "Well, did you do it, birthday boy? Did you get your Junior Ranger's badge?"

The adorable kid puffs out his chest, proudly displaying the wooden badge emblazoned with the park's logo.

"Congratulations! Wear it with pride," I say.

I dive into the speech I give to each party, and the ash blonde nods, staring ahead towards the area where I direct her to park before saying, "We'll sit up front and save you a seat."

"Thank you!" They drive away with Gregory leaning out of the window, looking over his shoulder, and waving at me.

After thirty more minutes of directing traffic, I walk down to the amphitheater, following the red lights lining the walkway. In the gloaming, I make out the dark forms of a packed crowd and four presenters on stage next to a bright, movie-theater-sized screen where PowerPoint slides provide a variable glow. Their dark profiles denote two tall, clean-cut men and two women. One woman wears her hair in a ponytail, and the other has a beautiful halo of mid-length curls. It's too dark to make out their faces.

The slide says they're here on behalf of the International Astronomical Union, discussing how stars, comets, and other celestial bodies get their names. It's a special presentation we don't normally offer. So, I haven't watched it before. The woman with the curls holds the mic, speaking as she points toward slides projected onto a large screen.

My eyes scan the front row until Gregory runs towards me, grabbing my hand. "We saved a spot for you," he whispers.

All I can say is the kid has incredible night vision because I can't see much of anything apart from the outlines of bodies. "Thank you, buddy."

I sandwich myself between Portia and the little boy, who starts chatting animatedly about his Pokemon card collection. His mom leans closer, whispering, "You can seriously tell him to quiet down whenever you like. He'll talk your ear off, just like his dad used to."

"Oh, are you all staying here together?"

"My husband was killed in action in Afghanistan."

My breath catches in my throat as her words hit me. "I'm so sorry for your loss."

"It's been tough," she says quietly. "Gregory was young when it happened. He doesn't have any memories of his father."

"Luna..." the little boy says, tugging on my sleeve.

"One moment," I whisper, lamenting the timing of his interruption.

"Gregory's father, Daniel, and I used to love this place. We came here every summer, so I try to keep up the tradition. It makes me feel closer to him."

I nod sadly, uncertain of how to respond.

"All I can say is never take for granted what you have. You never know when it will be gone. And always, always tell people how much you love them. The petty fights and disagreements mean nothing when they're gone. Fortunately, Daniel and I had an excellent last call, one I'll cherish for the rest of my life."

"That's so beau—"

"Luna!" Gregory practically yells, making his mother and I stop and stare at him. With a sickening feeling, I realize the entire audience is looking at us, including the four presenters on stage.

The boy hisses, "They're talking about you, Luna! That's what I've been trying to tell you."

Didn't Jessica say I wasn't presenting tonight? I look up at the stage, and the four figures look at me. I may not see their faces, but I feel their unmistakable gazes. This isn't the right place in the program to give my little artist-in-residence spiel. But whatever. I've done it so many times I could do it in my sleep. I probably have.

I stand up, but before I can stride to the stage, the crowd breaks into applause. One of the tall, clean-cut guys has the mic now, and he says, "Ladies and gentlemen, I'd like to introduce you to the woman who inspired the name for my most recent stellar discovery, Luna Solace."

I would recognize the deep, rich baritone anywhere. The crowd applauds, and my mind swirls. The three presenters who aren't speaking motion for me to come forward.

Am I dreaming or something? If so, I don't want to wake up until I hear that wonderful, familiar voice one more time...

Striding to the front, I stand before the guy with the microphone, staring incredulously at his face in the minimal glow of the projector. He's got short, neatly trimmed hair and a full beard. But my heart clamors at the familiar smell of the forest and those sky-blue eyes I'd know anywhere.

"Ledger?" My voice trembles as I lean in, scrutinizing his face in the dark. My hand comes up to his scarred side, feeling the familiar smooth skin but marveling at the ear, which my fingertips glide over, revealing a prosthetic, and the eyebrow and full beard. My fingertips stroke gently over his cheek, and my heart pounds, absorbing this new version of the man who's been on my mind unceasingly for seven months.

He leans down until his forehead rests on mine, whispering, "Hi, Snoop. I hope you'll forgive me for being a day late?"

A part of me wants to pull back and ask about the seven months I've waited. But Portia's warning runs through my head. Instead, I answer without hesitation, "Yes." Wrapping my arms tightly around his muscular frame, I hold him like I'm afraid he'll vanish into thin air. His warm, strong arms encircle me as I snuggle into his button-down cowboy shirt. Looking down, I make out the square toes of a pair of his tooled cowboy boots.

"I've dreamed about this moment for so long now. Please tell me it's real." My voice cracks at the end.

"It's real," he says breathlessly, stooping to kiss me as more cheers break out.

"And you named a star for me?"

"Yes, and I've never stopped thinking about you...or what I would do to find you again."

Letting go of his waist, I step back slightly, absorbing his face as my hands come up to his hair. "But who are you? I barely recognize you."

He stares deeply into my eyes, his filling with tears as he says, "I'm working on being the man you deserve, and I swear I'll keep working on it for the rest of our lives."

He pulls me tightly into his arms, and I stand on my tiptoes, whispering in his right ear, "Starboy, I wanted you before you did any of this. Even when you were a grumpy, reclusive, overgrown cowboy-mountain-man."

"And that gave me the strength and resolve to try to become what you need...forever. If you'll have me?"

"Of course I will," I whisper, pressing into him as his warm, soft lips and velvety tongue claim me passionately. The other presenters take over, stepping in front of us to continue their talk, and Ledger pulls me behind the screen where we're shielded from the eyes of the national park visitors.

"I came here to tell you how much I love you, Angel, and that I want to spend the rest of my life with you. You don't have to decide anything tonight, and I don't want to put you on the spot. I mean, we should probably start with a date or two. But I do want you to think about me...about us for a lot longer than a blizzard or a dark sky program."

"You're all I want," I answer, tears flooding my cheeks.

"Are you sure?" he asks breathlessly.

"More than sure." I pull him towards me for another kiss, starved for his smell, taste, voice, feel, and warmth...everything about him. He chuckles, his voice raw, clutching me with the same desperation. "Not only am I sure, cowboy, it's written in the stars, thanks to you."

"Thanks to God," he corrects quietly. "I was so furious with Him after my injuries that I couldn't see any of His gifts or blessings in my life. Because of my stubbornness and stupidity, I almost missed out on His most precious gift of all—you. Only after you left did I have time to reflect and realize finding you in the road in the blizzard was an inexplicable miracle. You really are my angel."

"And you're my miracle," I reply, smiling warmly as I palm his cheeks. "You saved me from the blizzard, and you've filled my heart with more love than I ever thought possible." Ledger closes the distance between us, tenderly kissing me as the starry night envelopes us in eternity.

If you loved Ledger & Luna's romance in *My Starry Valentine*, then you'll love Declan & Samantha's story in *My Grumpy Boss Valentine*.

CHECK IT OUR HERE

Find all the books in the Valentine's Sweethearts series at:

VALENTINE'S SWEETHEARTS FULL SERIES

৯.

Did you enjoy *My Starry Valentine?* If so, please review this book on Amazon, Goodreads, and Bookbub. Your feedback is greatly appreciated!

Amazon
Goodreads
Bookbub

Let's stay in touch! You can sign up for my newsletter at **ebsilva.com,** and be sure to follow me on Amazon for news about upcoming books and my latest releases: **amazon.com/ author/ebsilva**

Also by E.B. Silva

Mistletoe Mismatch- Worlds collide mile-high in Colorado when a blizzard traps a single dad and widower who's given up on love with a jaded romance writer who wants to believe in forever. Can a little Christmas magic prove this mismatch is made in heaven?

A MISTLETOE KISSES ROMANCE
E.B. SILVA

About the Author

E.B. Silva writes sweet, clean contemporary romances with all the feels. Her stories feature gruff cowboys and mountain men and the sassy, quirky woman they fall head over heels for.

Favorite tropes include grumpy/sunshine, fake engagement, marriage of convenience, found family, and best friends to lovers.

If you like cozy small-town vibes, expansive mountain views, and lovable characters who always find happily ever afters with their soulmates, E.B. Silva's your girl. Satisfying, heartfelt HEAs guaranteed!

Head to E.B. Silva's website to never miss out on upcoming and new releases as well as freebies and deals: www.ebsilva.com.

- ⊙ instagram.com/authorebsilva
- ♪ tiktok.com/@authorebsilva
- ⨍ facebook.com/authorebsilva
- ⓐ amazon.com/author/ebsilva
- 𝐁𝐁 bookbub.com/books/my-starry-valentine-a-sweet-ex-military-mountain-man-romance-by-e-b-silva